THE DAVID HUME INSTITUTE 1992

PUBLIC BROADCASTERS:
ACCOUNTABILITY AND EFFICIENCY

THE DAVID HUME INSTITUTE 1992

PUBLIC BROADCASTERS: ACCOUNTABILITY AND EFFICIENCY

Robin Foster

EDINBURGH UNIVERSITY PRESS

Edinburgh University Press
22 George Square, Edinburgh

Typeset in Monotype Times from author generated discs
by BPCC-AUP Glasgow Ltd
Printed in Great Britain by BPCC-Aberdeen Ltd

A CIP record for this book is available from the British Library

ISBN 0 7486 0410 3

Contents

Foreword

With the approach of the review of the BBC's charter and the publication of a Government Green Paper on the subject, the future of public broadcasting has never been more topical. Robin Foster's thoughtful and thought-provoking analysis of the considerations which will need to be taken into account is a timely and weighty contribution to an important debate. Making telling use of the recent experiences of public broadcasting in other countries, and drawing on the techniques employed in the privatisation of public enterprises, he argues that public broadcasters need to clarify and articulate their objectives, and to demonstrate that the objectives, once stated, are being met. Certain objectives for public broadcasting in a changing world are proposed, taking particular account of the liberal economic perspective that the capacity of the broadcasting audience to make its own choices must be respected. This does not preclude a role for public broadcasting to cope with market failures, but it must be subjected to the criteria imposed by accountability and efficiency. Robin Foster argues that there is therefore a need for a regulatory framework to ensure a fair yet competitive market in the provision of broadcasting services.

As always, the views expressed in this Hume Paper are those of the author rather than those of The David Hume Institute, which has no collective view on policy questions, being a charitable and non-political organisation. It is, however, a pleasure to be able to bring forward such a clearly argued paper dealing with a field in which the Institute has already been much involved.

Hector L. MacQueen
Executive Director

Introduction

Public broadcasters are in many ways a great British invention. Since the BBC first started broadcasting, the 'BBC model' for providing public broadcasting has been adopted around the world. Public broadcasters[1] have provided mainstream entertainment, information and education for viewers and listeners in Australia and in Austria, in New Zealand and in Norway, and in many other countries. Over the years public broadcasters have helped preserve national unity at times of crisis, have provided vital and (at their best) impartial information at times of unsettling and rapid change, and have provided popular cultural reference points for a generation of viewers and listeners.

As we move well into the 1990s, however, the (mostly) friendly and supportive world in which public broadcasters have so far operated is changing rapidly. Competition for audiences is increasing as the airwaves are liberalised, and production costs are rising as new money pursues a limited supply of broadcasting talent. Almost every public broadcaster is having to find ways of stretching limited resources further, while facing intensifying political pressure to justify their use of scarce public funds. Questions are being asked not only about how well public broadcasters are running their affairs, but about the very reason for their continued existence. The BBC's forthcoming charter review is only one example of the widespread examination around the world of the activities and objectives of public broadcasters. In some countries fundamental changes have already occurred (for example the privatisation of France's TF1, and the creation of a new public broadcasting funding system in New Zealand). In others, changes are planned (for example, the privatisation of the Singapore Broadcasting Corporation). In all countries public broadcasters will have to address difficult issues and challenges in the years ahead.

This paper examines the important issues of accountability and efficiency of public broadcasters against this uncertain background, and assesses whether there are steps that public broadcasters can take to improve their chances of successfully adapting to change. In particular, the paper looks at the extent to which public broadcasters can increase their political and public support. A necessary condition, it is argued, is the development of more clearly stated objectives, and methods of demonstrating to the public that those objectives are being met. Some of the techniques developed in the regulation of privatised utilities and other public enterprises are used to illustrate the measures which might be adopted in the broadcasting market. Although much of the discussion is generally applicable to all public broadcasters, some of the measures examined would be of particular relevance to the future regulation of the BBC in the UK.

In Chapter 1, the environment in which public broadcasters will have to operate is outlined. In addition to competitive pressures, they will face problems associated with inherited high cost and inefficient organisational structures. Further decline in public broadcasters' audience shares is inevitable, and public broadcasters which rely on public funding will find it difficult to argue for real increases in their grants or licence fees. There will be a temptation to tackle these problems in a piecemeal way (and indeed many public broadcasters have already begun impressive programmes of internal restructuring). But in the longer term, a sound financial future for public broadcasters will depend on a more clearly defined and widely supported view of what public broadcasting should be concerned with. This will have implications for the size, structure, and nature of public broadcasters, and is a task which broadcasters and governments need to address with some urgency.

What *should* be the role of public broadcasters in the 1990s and beyond? Before deciding what public *broadcasters* should do, it is essential to decide what public *broadcasting* should be all about. (The two are not necessarily synonymous). Chapter 2 examines some of the options for redefining the objectives of public broadcasting, drawing on both economic and sociocultural perspectives. It concludes that value judgements concerning the role of public broadcasting, whether or not one agrees with them, provide inadequate guidance for deciding how many resources should be allocated to public broadcasting as a whole and to the different elements of public broadcasting. A more liberal economic view – that consumers will generally be the best judges of their own interests – appears to offer a better starting point for analysing what public broadcasting should be expected to provide. Governments, indeed, have often underestimated the ability of the public to make sensible choices about the types of broadcasting they would like to receive. While that assessment may have been soundly based in the early days of broadcasting, it now seems likely that audiences are much more sophisticated in their use and understanding of the broadcast media. The need for a benevolent guiding hand, directing our viewing and listening, is increasingly less obvious.

Nevertheless, even from a strict liberal economic perspective, market failures do provide a number of justifications for government intervention in broadcasting markets, to prevent concentration of private ownership, to ensure that certain types of programme are provided and perhaps to encourage an efficient level of risk taking and innovation. But developments in broadcasting, especially the rapid emergence of new satellite and cable channels, are reducing the importance of these rationales.

There is therefore a need to reassess which services and programmes are unlikely to be provided by the market, but which nevertheless are of value to individuals or to society as a whole (and which, by implication, might justify public funding). Indications are that public funding should support a narrower or more carefully targeted range of programmes and services than has hitherto been the case. But any decision to alter radically the scale and scope of public broadcasting needs to be well informed by the views and preferences of viewers and listeners, which could provide useful guidelines for government policy and broadcasters' strategies.

Governments also need to assess whether public broadcasters provide the best conduit for government intervention in broadcasting markets. It is clearly insufficient to argue that public broadcasters have been successful in the past. A stronger case might be made in terms of the positive impact public broadcasters have on risk taking and innovation, and the importance of providing a critical mass of creative talent. But these benefits are only worth supporting as long as they are not swamped by bureaucratic inefficiency and corporate arrogance. In this context, measures to reduce costs and increase accountability will strengthen the case for public broadcasters' continued existence into the next century.

In Chapter 3, the issue of improved accountability is assessed in greater detail. There is a general trend for governments to insist that public enterprises deliver value for money, and are more accountable to their users. As part of this movement, public enterprises are being asked to enter into more formal service contracts or agreements, and to publish information about the level and quality of service they provide. Public broadcasters are unlikely to be able to escape these developments and, indeed, may be able to turn them to their advantage.

The problems in formulating broadcasting service contracts are well known, and can only be partly overcome. But enough can be accomplished to make the exercise worthwhile. Recognising the need for clearer contracts and service performance indicators does not solve the problem of how to implement them. Nor does it provide guidance on the optimal service levels required. As a general principle, though, contracted broadcasting services should draw their legitimacy from the nature and scope of public broadcasting that the general public (the licence fee payers) would like to support. Likewise, service quality indicators should concentrate on measuring public approval for the service and programmes produced. Formalised contracts will help ensure that important questions concerning the future scope of public broadcasters' activities are properly addressed. It may be possible to 'decouple' the public service aspects of public broadcasters' output from the more commercial elements, creating a more transparent use of public funds.

Chapter 4 turns to the question of efficiency. Whatever the remit given to public broadcasters, there is an unanswerable case for ensuring they produce their service as efficiently as possible. This means the encouragement of internal productive efficiency, and also the pursuit of efficient allocation of resources between competing broadcasters and between broadcasting and other uses.

Various mechanisms could be used to provide public broadcasters with effective efficiency incentives. One option is a licence fee indexation formula, modelled on the type of price-cap regulation typically used in the UK to control the prices of regulated utilities. Care would need to be taken to ensure that such a formula did not produce adverse service quality incentives or prevent necessary capital investment. Indeed, providing adequate efficiency incentives while at the same time promoting service quality is one of the most difficult issues facing broadcasting regulators. It would generally be preferable to fix the licence fee formula for a number of years, to provide public broadcasters with greater funding certainty and freedom from more frequent government intervention. A related option would be the creation of an independent broadcasting regulator to monitor and control the public broadcaster's activities.

Public broadcasters' internal efficiency incentives could be improved by the establishment of a system of internal markets and the contracting out of some services. At the very least, such action would allow broadcasters to acquire detailed information on industry-wide production costs, which will provide a useful benchmark for their own performance.

More radical use of market mechanisms could yield the biggest efficiency gains, but would also provide public broadcasters with their biggest challenge. Such mechanisms might include competition for public funds (via an Arts Council of the Air, perhaps) and the increased exploitation by public broadcasters of subscription revenue. Both could call into question the rationale for continuing with the existing institutional framework for the provision of public broadcasting.

In the final chapter, the paper suggests two options for the future of public broadcasters: a '*core service*' *option*, in which public broadcasters concentrate on filling in the gaps left by the private sector; and a '*wider service*' *option*, in which public broadcasters provide a much broader programming service in direct competition with private operators. Both options, it is argued, have their drawbacks, demonstrating the difficult policy choices facing public broadcasters and governments alike.

The first option in effect accepts that the scale and scope of public broadcasting should be much more narrowly focused in future, and that public broadcasters should be asked to provide this level of service and no more. The danger of this option is that it might result in increasing marginalisation of the broadcaster's services and a consequent funding squeeze. Public broadcasters could counter this by seeking greater public legitimacy, and by a demonstration of real accountability, although the level of public support they will receive is uncertain.

The second option, which by implication extends the activities of public broadcasters beyond a narrow interpretation of public broadcasting, has far greater resource requirements. It is probably inevitable that public broadcasters with such a wide remit will need a relatively free hand to exploit commercial revenue sources to supplement public funding. It will be desirable for those public broadcasters, especially those already financed in part by advertising and subscription, to be set commercial financial objectives, and to be given much greater freedom to implement their commercial strategies. They would be subject to well defined and funded public service contracts for their 'non-commercial' broadcasting output, but would be free from direct government intervention in their remaining areas of activity. If this second option is chosen, a logical extension would be the eventual privatisation of the public broadcaster.

A 'middle way' exists, in which public broadcasters attempt to enhance their revenues by incremental changes in their programming strategy and/or by exploiting new revenue sources. This path is a tricky one to pursue and, for some broadcasters, could end in a cul de sac. In particular, it might only postpone, rather than solve, the problems identified in the main body of this paper.

The BBC is in a rather different position from that of the majority of its public counterparts elsewhere in the world in that it depends almost wholly on public funding. (Ironically, it is among the more commercially orientated of all the major public broadcasters). Although it does need to rethink its main objectives and more clearly differentiate its services from those provided by the private sector, and although it is likely to find it difficult to persuade governments to increase licence fee payments significantly, the BBC is less exposed than some of its fellow public broadcasters to the effects of an audience and revenue share squeeze. Scope clearly exists for the BBC to extend its commercial activities, but they will need to be carefully 'ring-fenced' from its publicly funded core service. It is less obvious that privatisation of the BBC would yield significant benefits, however, unless it were accompanied by a major change in the extent to which the BBC is allowed to exploit advertising and subscription finance, which in turn would affect the whole UK broadcasting market. The risk of such large scale disruption is only worth taking if privatisation seems to be the only way of unlocking the BBC's immense potential as a world force in broadcasting and as a major UK export earner. But the costs of privatisation are also likely to be large.

Whether or not privatisation is on the political agenda, an assessment of the benefits and costs of a more commercially oriented BBC should be a central part of the forthcoming charter review. Also important will be a strengthened regulatory framework, which should encourage the BBC to exploit profitable commercial opportunities, while safeguarding the public from paying for the BBC's commercial failures and other broadcasters from unfair competition.

My sincere thanks are due to all my colleagues at NERA with whom I have worked on broadcasting projects over the past five years. In particular, I would like to thank Dermot Glynn for his comments on an earlier draft and, not least, for allowing me the time to write this paper.

1 A Changing World

Revolutionary Change

In the 70 years since the BBC provided its first regular service, the world in which broadcasters have operated has significantly changed. Technology has brought immense service quality improvements (stereo sound, colour television, live worldwide satellite links and many more). Radio and television production techniques and styles have evolved and improved. However, what has hitherto been evolutionary change is now being replaced by revolutionary change. Fundamental shifts in the relationship between viewers/listeners and broadcasters are taking place, largely driven by two forces: a proliferation of television channels and radio stations, and the emergence of new methods of direct payment for the broadcasting media, especially television. The industry's structure and its cost base are at the same time being reassessed. Broadcasting is entering a new period of development, and public broadcasters will be affected by these changes as profoundly as their commercial counterparts.

Increased Competition

In their early years, public broadcasters often faced no competition from private broadcasters. The BBC was challenged by one rival commercial (private) television channel from 1955 onwards, and (apart from 'pirate' radio stations in the 1960s) by private radio stations only from 1973 onwards. Other European public broadcasters were protected from private competition for even longer. The first private television channels in Germany, for example, did not begin broadcasting until 1984; in Spain there was no competition until 1990. Even the new private operators were often constrained by so-called public service programming obligations, which helped limit the frequency of head-to-head battles for audiences. In the UK, and in some other countries, competition for revenues was avoided by dividing the market into two. On one side stood the public broadcasters, funded by the taxpayer, on the other stood the private operators, financed by the advertisers. For the most part, broadcasting markets were characterised by a process of incremental change, carefully regulated by the relevant government authorities.

Radio was the first part of the broadcasting market to experience the real force of widespread competition. Partly because enough radio frequencies were available for the establishment of local radio stations throughout

Europe, and partly because the capital and operating costs of local radio are relatively low compared with potential revenues, pressure built up from the private radio lobby for a relaxation of government constraints on competition. Protests from the radio audience helped too. The success of private radio stations in the 1960s, including unlicensed pirate operators, clearly showed that public radio broadcasters were not catering well for a large section of the potential radio audience. There are now over 5,000 national and local radio stations operating throughout Europe. In many markets, private radio broadcasters have a far higher share of the listening audience than public broadcasters. Public broadcasters, however, still have the edge in terms of the range of radio programming offered. They typically offer speech-based programming (drama, news-current affairs etc), classical music, popular music and programmes for special and minority interests. Private stations (driven by hard economics) almost invariably provide a mix of recorded music and chat.

In the mid to late 1980s, the force of competition began to spread into the television market. The first signs of this were in terrestrial television. At the start of the 1980s most European countries still had a limited number of television channels, the majority of which were run by public broadcasters. Only four private commercial services operated in the whole of Europe. It was clear from experience elsewhere – most notably in the US – that large amounts of money could be made by operating private commercial television channels. It was also clear that viewers (voters) generally welcomed more television choice. The interests of prospective private television operators and of the politicians coincided, and a will was found to make available the necessary radio frequencies to allow new channels to enter the market. Examples include RTL Plus (Germany), Canale 5 (Italy) and La Cinq (France). Now there are over 20 national private terrestrial channels in operation in Europe, competing against 39 public broadcasting channels.[1]

More important, though, were the technological developments taking place which would allow many more television channels to be delivered to viewers. Terrestrial television transmission requires substantial amounts of the radio spectrum – spectrum which is also highly sought by other users, such as mobile telephone operators or by defence organisations. In the absence of technology to squeeze more television into the same amount of radio spectrum, there is an inevitable limit to the amount of television which can be made available terrestrially. Delivery of television signals by cable and satellite has completely changed this picture.

The development of cable systems by-passes the radio spectrum constraint, by providing a delivery mechanism for much larger numbers of television channels (some of the newer US systems, for example, provide capacity for over 100 channels). By 1992, cable systems were well advanced in many European countries, providing a significant increase in television choice to those households with access to a cable network.

The emergence of direct-to-home (DTH) satellite broadcasting has been the second major building block of competition in television. DTH satellites provide a relatively cheap method of distribution for television signals (a single transponder on the Astra satellite, for example, costs £4–5m a year to lease, and sends a signal to most of western Europe). They also have multi-channel capacity (each of Astra's satellites can now deliver 16 channels). Households prepared to pay the (not insubstantial) cost of buying or renting a satellite receiver dish can obtain access to a large number of extra television services. In most European countries there is now a large choice of channels available to everyone, delivered either by cable or DTH satellite, in addition to those television channels available terrestrially. In 1991, just over 20 per cent of households in Europe were already receiving a multiplicity of television channels via cable or satellite. In Germany the figure was 40 per cent, in the Netherlands 80 per cent. Over 60 different television channels are now available via satellite across Europe, and the total is steadily increasing.

Declining Public Broadcaster Audiences

Not surprisingly, audiences for radio stations and television channels operated by public broadcasters have declined. Figure 1.1, for example, shows that public television's audience share has dropped by 30 per cent since 1980. The decline in some countries has been even more dramatic. In Spain, for example, RTVE was the near-monopoly public television broadcaster until 1990. Three new private channels (two financed by advertising, one by subscription) were introduced in that year. Two years later they are regularly winning 30 per cent of viewers. In Germany, RTL Plus and Sat 1 (which use a mix of terrestrial, cable and satellite delivery) account for over 20 per cent of viewers, five years after their introduction.

In the UK, the BBC suffered its first major decline in its television audience

Share of total viewing in Europe

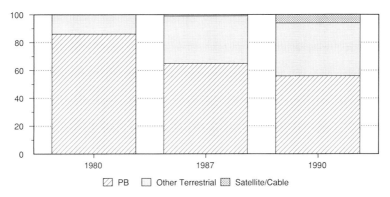

Based on France, Germany, Italy, Spain, UK
Source: NERA

FIGURE 1.1   PUBLIC BROADCASTERS' TV VIEWING SHARE HAS FALLEN BY 30% SINCE 1980

share in the 1950s after the start of ITV. More recently, though, it has started to come under increasing pressure from the new satellite channels, which now attract around one-third of viewing hours in those households which can receive satellite signals. Viewing of BBC channels in 'satellite' households has dipped to 30 per cent according to some surveys (compared with a 45 per cent overall market share) and BBC2 has performed particularly badly. As satellite or cable subscription increases, so the BBC's overall television audience share is bound to decline further. Projections prepared by NERA, for example, indicate an overall BBC audience share (for two channels) of around 40 per cent by 1995, falling further by 2000.

Giving Audiences What They Want

The new television channels and radio stations have been able to win audiences by providing popular programming. They are driven by commercial rather than public service principles, so have no reason not to offer the programming that will maximise their profits. A brief review of the successful private terrestrial television channels shows that their schedules are packed with game shows, light entertainment, situation comedies and popular dramas. High budget programming is needed in the schedules from time-to-time to persuade viewers to tune in to the channel. This might comprise local dramas, entertainment spectaculars, or major sports events. But average hourly programming costs are relatively low, and to keep average costs down, they often rely heavily on imported product, mainly from the US.

Compared with public service channels, the new private operators broadcast far fewer current affairs, documentary, cultural and minority interest programmes. The contrast is shown in Figure 1.2.

Satellite or cable-only channels are somewhat different again. The increased number of available channels and reduced distribution costs have allowed operators to pursue greater market segmentation than has ever been possible for terrestrial television broadcasters. Their programming is often aimed at particular sub-sectors of the total audience. This trend first become evident in radio, where specialist stations (such as those catering for adult-oriented rock music, country music or light classical music) are now common in the US and in other developed radio markets. Television economics made such segmentation less attractive until the advent of lower-cost cable and satellite distribution systems. Helped by the new delivery methods a range of specialised new channels has emerged in Europe, including several film channels, channels devoted to sports, and channels showing news, pop music, comedy, children's programmes and nature documentaries. Even more specialised channels are available on some cable systems. For example, in the UK an Indian channel, Indra Dhhnush, is shown by some cable networks. In the US, the range of available cable channels is even wider, although it seems unlikely that television (because of its cost structure) will ever reproduce the range and diversity of choice available in the print media.

By the middle of the 1990s, viewers and listeners will therefore have a much

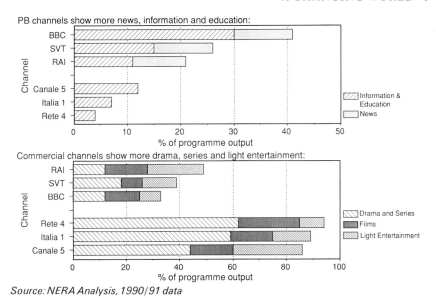

Source: NERA Analysis, 1990/91 data

FIGURE 1.2   THERE ARE MARKED DIFFERENCES BETWEEN PUBLIC BROADCASTER AND
COMMERCIAL TV CHANNELS

wider choice of television channels and radio stations than ever before. Some of the output will be unashamedly down-market. Some will be low-cost programming with little artistic or cultural merit. Some will be third or fourth-run material, probably bought from the US. However, there are also likely to be channels showing premium films, well-produced news, sports and children's programmes, and several other specialist subjects. Programming will be geared towards what mass audiences want (or in some cases, what large minority audiences want). It is against this background that governments have to determine the future objectives for public broadcasters.

Competition for Revenues

Competition for audiences has also meant competition for revenues. One feature of restricted competition in broadcasting in the 1970s and 1980s was that those operators lucky enough to have broadcasting licences – including the public broadcasters – made a very good living. Fuelled by overall economic growth, television advertising grow rapidly in real terms generating large profits for the few private broadcasters and for those public broadcasters partly financed by advertising. Public broadcasters also often benefitted from a rising total licence fee income, caused by a switch to colour television sets (with generally a higher licence fee) and a trend to smaller households (more licence fee-payers). As a result, between 1980 and 1990, public broadcasters' revenues in the major European markets increased by about 40 per cent in real terms. Some of the broadcasters' income was channelled back to government in the form of special taxes. Some was invested in more expensive programming or longer broadcast hours. Some contributed to industry-wide cost inflation as the price of scarce resources was bid up.

In the 1990s, broadcasting revenues will continue to grow, but there will be considerable variation in the rates of growth achieved by different countries and from different revenue sources. Across Europe there is still scope for further expansion in the television advertising market. There are quite wide variations in Europe in the proportion of GDP represented by television advertising, for example. Television advertising accounts for 0.5 per cent of GDP in Spain, but only 0.1 per cent in Germany. Although some of this variation reflects cultural and regulatory differences,[2] there is likely to be a closing of the gap between the lowest and the highest markets. In those markets, such as the UK, where television advertising is already quite high, growth will still occur, but at a more modest rate than in the 1980s. For example, NERA projects that the total UK television advertising market will increase by just under 5 per cent a year in real terms for the rest of the 1990s. By 2000, the total UK market will then be around £2,600m, compared with £1,700m in 1991.

The great difference between the 1990s and previous decades, however, is that the television market is now much more open to entry. It is much less likely that any individual private operator will be able to earn above normal profits for any sustained period of time. It is more likely that new channels will enter the market, attracted by the prospect of capturing some of the potential revenues. Hence, while total advertising revenues generated by the private television sector may be substantially higher in real terms in 2000 than they are now, individual channels may be doing less well. It is not yet clear whether the market will reach any sort of equilibrium, and whether that would involve a large number of low-cost channels, each taking a small share of the market, or a small number of high-cost channels, each taking a substantial share.

Public broadcasters dependent in part on advertising for their funding will not be able to take full advantage of the likely growth in television advertising. As competition increases for the audiences sought by advertisers, public broadcasters will be handicapped by their public service obligations. They will be unable fully to match the popular programming shown by their terrestrial competitors, nor will they be able to offer such fine market segmentation as their cable/satellite rivals. Moreover, some governments place extra restrictions on advertising carried by public channels. This further limits their ability to operate effectively in an increasingly competitive market.

Public broadcasters dependent on public funding for some or all of their income will be in an equally difficult position. Although private broadcasters in a more liberalised market might fail in their attempt to generate extra revenues (their rivals might simply be better) at least they will have the chance to try. Public broadcasters, faced with governments reluctant to increase the burden of taxation, will find it difficult to secure real increases in public funding. Such increases will be especially difficult to obtain if, at the same time, public broadcasters' audiences are steadily declining and the range of programming choice available from private broadcasters is rapidly increasing.

As Figure 1.3 shows, licence fee income has already substantially declined as a proportion of total revenues earned by broadcasters. It is hard to see an end to this trend.

Increasing Importance of Direct Payment

Advertising and licence fees are not, of course, the only potential revenue sources. Of particular importance for the next ten years will be the increased acceptance by consumers of direct payment for television.[3] A feature of television is that it has, until recently, been relatively expensive to exclude viewers from receiving signals (for example by encoding transmissions and providing viewers with a decoding device). Without such a system, it is impossible to charge viewers for a television service (unless, like the licence fee, payment is compulsory for those with a receiver). Now, however, encryption and billing systems (to administer subscriptions) are available at a cost which makes subscription television a viable proposition for some types of programming.

Consumers already pay substantial amounts for video entertainment. Table

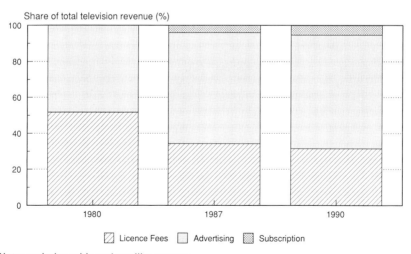

Note: excludes cable and satellite revenue
Based on France, Germany, Italy, Spain and UK

FIGURE 1.3   ADVERTISING REVENUE HAS BECOME MORE IMPORTANT IN EUROPE THAN LICENCE FEE INCOME OVER THE 1980s

1.1 shows how much is spent in Europe on video rentals and purchases, for example. In addition, subscription (pay) television is growing in importance. Average spend on pay TV in Europe is currently about £15 per pay TV household per month. In the US, about 30 per cent of all households pay in the region of £10 a month for a basic cable package. This usually consists of a mix of general and themed channels. A further 30 per cent pays £19 a month for a package of basic and premium cable channels – usually including recent release films and major sports events. In the UK, those households subscribing to cable or satellite channels already spend up to £25 a month in addition to any licence fee payments.

These figures should be placed in the context of an average European licence fee payment of less than £7.00 per month. The fact that consumers are prepared to pay such large amounts to obtain certain types of programming (generally recent films and major sports events) or to increase their choice of channels arguably indicates the failure of traditional broadcasters to cater for the preferences of – at least some sectors of – their audiences. If subscription television in Europe is eventually as successful as it is in the US, income in the order of £10 billion a year could be generated. This is roughly the total amount currently raised from licence fees, and could represent about 30 per cent of all broadcasting revenues by 2000. Consideration needs to be given to whether public broadcasters can tap into this potential source of new funding, and whether it is consistent with their public service obligations.

Pressures on Costs

Public broadcasters face a further issue when dealing with future competition. Almost without exception they have a significant cost disadvantage. Public

TABLE 1.1   MONTHLY SPENDING ON VIDEO SOFTWARE IN 1991

| | Average monthly expenditure per VCR home (£) | | |
	% of TV homes with VCR	Rental	Sell-through	Total
Belgium	50.7	1.36	1.41	2.77
Denmark	45.7	2.14	0.94	3.08
France	51.6	0.60	2.79	3.39
Germany	58.4	1.71	0.78	2.49
Greece	30.4	1.32	—	1.32
Ireland	55.0	5.78	1.61	7.39
Italy	31.1	1.32	3.08	4.40
Netherlands	51.9	7.20	5.69	12.89
Portugal	32.2	2.79	0.81	3.60
Spain	48.7	2.38	0.76	3.14
UK	71.5	2.74	1.85	4.59

Source: Screen Digest, NERA

broadcasters have evolved over time as vertically integrated organisations, responsible for everything from making their programmes to operating their transmission system. All or most locally-produced programming was made in-house, calling for substantial investment in studio capacity. In those countries where competition was allowed only recently, little production capacity existed outside the public broadcasting sector. As a result, the various components of the public broadcasting process (studios, technical support, other support services such as wardrobe, make-up, programme production, transmission) have not had to face competing sources of supply. Programme producers have always used the public broadcaster's own facilities and technicians. There was no other option open to them. There have also been few external benchmarks against which the performance of the organisation as a whole or of its various constituent parts could be measured. A lack of comparative information has meant that governments have found it difficult to judge whether public broadcasters have been justified in their periodic requests for increases in public funding. This combination of factors, coupled with a 'public service' (as opposed to 'commercial') management philosophy, has greatly reduced the incentives for public service broadcasters to control costs and improve efficiency.

Some of the older private broadcasters, apparently awash with profits, were for a time similarly relaxed about productive efficiency. But the new broadcasters, especially the cable and satellite television channel operators, are of a different breed. Unless they control costs, they will fail. The start-up costs of a new channel are high. Until a critical mass of viewers is achieved, advertising revenues or subscription income will not cover operating costs. Given this, the new private operators have sought ways to reduce costs dramatically. They have much lower staffing levels, fewer studios and other fixed costs, and make greater use of independent (external) producers than public broadcasters. They avoid heavy management overheads, and agree to big budget programming only when convinced it will produce a direct return in higher ratings or longer-term subscription to their channel. The average hourly direct programme costs of public broadcasters are typically £50,000 or greater. Some of the new private operators work on the basis of average programming costs of much less than half this amount.

Because of their programme mix and reluctance to rely too much on imported material, public broadcasters will probably always have a higher average hourly programme cost than some of the new broadcasters. Moreover, the cost disadvantage of public broadcasters has been compounded in some countries by government intervention to encourage the development of an independent production sector. Some public broadcasters now have to meet quotas of programming sourced from independents. But if this leaves their own facilities and other resources under-utilised, there is likely to be a significant cost penalty until production resources can be scaled down. Other 'regulatory' cost penalties might include obligations on public broadcasters to broadcast in minority languages, to provide financial support for orchestras and other cultural activities, and to provide local or regional radio and television coverage.

An additional cost pressure, likely to increase further in the 1990s, is that associated with competitive bids for scarce creative resources, acquired programmes, or rights to broadcast major sports events. Although the broadcasting market should, in the medium term, adjust to revenue growth and increased competition (more skilled resources will be attracted into broadcasting), there will always be keen competition for highly-valued scarce resources. These will include popular television performers, successful imported programmes, and the broadcast rights to major films, sports and other events. Private broadcasters will be anxious to obtain such resources because of the potential pay-off in terms of audiences and revenues. They are especially valuable to those operators who need to build audiences quickly in view of their high start-up costs. Faced with this intense competition, public broadcasters will find it increasingly difficult to stay in the race for high-profile programming. If they do stay in the race, it will be at the risk of starving other programming of necessary funds. It will also be at the risk of alienating public and political support because of the high payments involved.

A View of the Future

As we move towards the mid 1990s, therefore, public broadcasters face several significant potential problems. Their audience shares, in both television and radio, are declining, and further decline seems inevitable. Those which rely partly on advertising revenue will receive a declining share of the advertising cake. Those which rely on public funding will find it difficult to argue for real increases in their grants or licence fees. Perhaps the most important future source of television funding – direct payment – is as yet largely unexploited by public broadcasters. While resources are likely to be squeezed, costs are in danger of escalating. Public broadcasters have inherited high-cost and inefficient structures from their earlier days, and are now faced with competition from leaner and more profit-oriented private operators. Competition for scarce programme resources will push up the costs of some important areas of programming, an increase which public broadcasters will find hard to fund.

There will be a temptation to deal with each of those problems in a piecemeal way. For example, it might be possible for public broadcasters to address their declining audiences by a modest shift in their schedules towards programming of a more popular appeal. A revenue shortfall could be tackled by governments allowing a small increase in (or the introduction of) advertising sales. Judicious use could be made of sponsorship to generate commercial revenues in the absence of advertising. Efforts could be made to introduce better financial information and more efficient internal control of costs. Alliances could be sought to share the high costs of acquiring premium programming.

Some or all of these measures are being adopted or considered by most public broadcasters in Europe. But in the longer term, a sound financial future for public broadcasters will depend on a more clearly defined and widely supported view of what public broadcasters should be concerned with. This will have implications for the size, structure and nature of public broadcasting, and is a task which broadcasters and governments need to address with some urgency.

2 Redefining the Rationale

Back to First Principles

A good starting point in determining the future role of public broadcasters is to examine the various rationales for their existence. Two questions need to be answered. First, what is public *broadcasting* ? and, second, are public *broadcasters* the best means of delivering public broadcasting efficiently to viewers and listeners? Answering these questions is less easy than it might first appear, for different governments at different times have had their own specific reasons for creating and supporting public broadcasters. Broadcasters themselves have also done much to advance rationales for public broadcasting which naturally support their own existence. The development of public broadcasters and public broadcasting are inextricably linked, so it is difficult to disentangle the two questions. The distinguished economist R. H. Coase noted a quarter of a century ago that broadcasting policy developed in a world:

> in which ignorance, prejudice, and mental confusion, encouraged rather than dispelled by the political organisation, exert a strong influence on policy making.[1]

A review of the current activities of public broadcasters around the world, however, reveals a remarkable unanimity of purpose. Most governments ask their public broadcasters to:

- provide *universality* of service provision and, linked to this, the provision of services of the same technical quality to all;
- cater for a *variety and diversity* of interests and tastes, usually including popular as well as specialist tastes;
- provide programmes which *inform and educate* , such as news, current affairs, documentaries, cultural and other programmes of educational value;
- cater for '*minorities*' – this may be expressed in terms of requirements for local production reflecting the culture, language and lifestyle of the country or community in question.

Is this enough to define public broadcasting? Such objectives are necessarily based on value judgements about the importance of specified social goals (for example of ensuring a voice for ethnic minorities, or supporting local creative talent) and differ in perceived importance from country to country. They partly originate in the view, which was prevalent when broadcasting first began, that radio and television have substantial and indeed unrivalled power to influence their audiences' opinions and values. The Sykes Committee (1923), the first of many inquiries on the subject of broadcasting in the UK, concluded that:

> the control of such a potential power over public opinion and the life of the nation ought to remain with the State.

Even when broadcasting markets were later partially opened to private sector competition, it was still felt important to retain a state-owned broadcaster to uphold public service values. In some countries, public broadcasters have been closely controlled and influenced by government. Government controls the purse strings and influences programme and editorial policy. In these cases, the public broadcaster is encouraged to be the 'Voice of the Nation', although that voice is in reality the voice of the government. In other countries including the UK, the public broadcaster is less directly influenced by government, but is still seen as a national institution often reflecting, promoting and protecting national culture and traditions.

'Universality' has long been held to be a vital aspect of public broadcasting. All viewers and listeners, including those in the most remote areas, should be able to receive broadcasts. Furthermore, broadcasts should be made available to all viewers on the same terms. The aim, presumably, is to promote national/regional identity, and social cohesion. The Annan Committee,[2] for example, argued that broadcasting is unique and different from other forms of communications because of its mass audience:

> Radio, as well as television, possesses the unique quality of addressing simultaneously the greater part of the population .... At a time when people worry that society is fragmenting, broadcasting welds it together. It links people, gives the mass audience common topics of conversation, makes them realise that, in experiencing similar emotions, they all belong to the same nation.

An extension of this concept is the view (quite often advanced by broadcasters themselves) that it is the duty of public service broadcasters to cover all events of national significance. In the UK, for example, these might include coverage of general elections, royal weddings (or divorces), and important sports events such as the FA and Scottish Cup Finals.

Ironically, as the number of television channels, and radio stations increases, and as each broadcaster receives a smaller share of the total audience, then broadcasting is likely to become less important and powerful than it was considered to be when first introduced. It is less likely that any single broadcaster, assuming there is a multiplicity of choice, will have a monopoly in audience manipulation and influence. There will be far fewer shared experiences for the mass audience.

The cultural and educational role of public broadcasting has been much debated. The Annan Committee argued that the role of broadcasters is:

> to enlarge people's interests, to convey to them new choices and possibilities in life, this is what broadcasting ought to try to achieve. Sir Huw Wheldon, with remarkable brevity, has said that programmes should 'create delight and insight'. This sums up our views.

It is fair to characterise these views as being representative of mainstream thinking on the objectives of public broadcasting for much of the past fifty or so years. They were (and often still are) widely held by the political and broadcasting establishment, and reflect a paternalistic concern with 'enriching' the cultural experiences of viewers and listeners.

The fact that the same elements commonly occur in the output of public broadcasters around the world however, does not mean they satisfactorily define what public service broadcasters should be doing. Nor does it mean they are the 'right' elements for the future. One difficulty with basing policy decisions on value judgements of this kind is that they give little guidance to policy makers on how many resources to devote to public broadcasting, and how to allocate those resources between competing claims for support. At some point the gain from extending the range of programmes available must be offset by the loss in output elsewhere. It follows that the provision of programmes which are liked by one group will have deprived some other group of programmes they would have liked. It is possible to agree in broad terms with the value judgements, while also accepting that they do not, in themselves, provide sufficient justification for substantial public funding of broadcasting or guidelines on how funding should be distributed between types of programme service.

An Economic Rationale

A different starting point is to examine the rationale a liberal economist would use for public intervention in broadcasting. At its most basic level, such an approach would suggest that provision of broadcasting services should be entrusted to private markets, and that intervention by government should only take place where broadcasting markets are not working effectively. The proposition that economic principles might be applied to public broadcasting is not new but it is still regarded as controversial in some circles. Broadcasting is too important to be left to the market place, it is argued. But economic systems are generally accepted to have a vital role to play in the provision of most other goods and services and it is not obvious why broadcasting should be the exception.

Economic market systems exist to provide a means through which producers have an incentive to supply goods and services that consumers want and are willing to pay for. They reconcile competing demands for resources via the price mechanism. Intervention may be needed to ensure that enough competition exists, that everyone observes some basic rules of the game, that social costs and benefits are internalised in private transactions, and also to ensure income for people without the necessary means to support themselves. But generally the value judgement is made that consumers should be left to decide for themselves what they wish to consume, and that the function of supply is to benefit the consumer.[3] Abstracting for a moment from the mechanism by which transactions might take place in broadcasting, this boils down to accepting that viewers and listeners are usually the best judges of their own interest.

The Peacock report[4] was an influential advocate of the importance of taking note of 'what the public wants' or 'consumer sovereignty'. Peacock noted that it is a good general principle that any service to the public should be designed to promote its satisfaction, and that the public is best served if able to buy the amount of the service required from suppliers who compete for custom through price and quality. The Peacock report's central finding was that:

> British broadcasting should move towards a sophisticated market system based on consumer sovereignty. That is a system which recognises that viewers and listeners are the best ultimate judges of their own interests, which they can best satisfy if they have the option of purchasing the broadcasting services they require from as many alternative sources of supply as possible.[5]

This assumes, of course, that the consumer is the best judge of his/her own interests, but this simple proposition has met with much resistance over the years. Several arguments have been used to oppose it. For example:

- consumers can only make effective choices if they either (a) have enough information about what they are buying or (b) can 'learn by doing';
- consumers do not automatically choose the pattern of goods and services which is in their best interests.

The Pilkington Committee, for example, offered the following view:

> Because in principle the possible range of subject matter is inexhaustible, all of it can never be presented, nor can the public know what the range is. So the broadcaster must explore it, and choose from it first. This might be called 'giving a lead': but it is not the lead of the autocratic or arrogant. It is the proper exercise of responsibility by public authorities duly constituted as trustees for the public interest.

Broadcasters will decide, not the public. (How broadcasters should decide, how they will get the information on which to base their decision, and what connection this will have with the public interest are not clear.)

These arguments no longer appear particularly convincing. Consumers generally have access to a wealth of published information about most programmes. The costs to the consumer of making an 'incorrect' choice are not high. Concerning the ability of consumers to choose what is in their best interests, it would surely be better to educate consumers in making their own choices and to provide them with good information with which to make those choices rather than to select the programmes for them. Indeed, arguments which suggest the consumer is unable to choose ignore the great changes that have taken place in the way people use television and radio in recent years. Viewers are more likely to pick and choose between programmes. They are much less likely to remain with the same service all evening. They use VCRs to record programmes and watch them at different times ('time-shift' viewing). Over 70 per cent of UK households now have VCRs. They use remote controls to sample different programmes and to avoid watching advertising breaks. Radios now often have pre-set tuning, allowing listeners to hop easily between stations. In other words, consumers are much more sophisticated in their use of broadcast media than some theories would suggest.

While there was some justification for broadcasters exercising judgement on behalf of viewers and listeners as long as the available choice of television and radio was limited, such justifications must become much weaker as the range and diversity of broadcasting increases. Viewers and listeners have in the past been prevented from giving full expression to their own preferences for a number of reasons, notably including limited channel choice. They cannot develop their tastes and preferences unless they have access to a wide range of alternative forms and sources of programmes. However, as the range of television and radio programming available to audiences increases, so there is less justification for broadcasting authorities to select programming on the public's behalf.

A more effective means of improving the exercise of consumer choice, indeed, is to help ensure that there is much greater freedom of entry into broadcasting markets. This implies a need for governments to reduce regulatory entry barriers, and also to ensure that existing operators do not create their own entry barriers via increased horizontal and vertical integration, or by a range of possible anti-competitive acts (such as for example, the acquisition of long-term exclusive rights for key programming material).

Market Failures

Acceptance of the 'public knows best' principle does not rule out the need for public intervention in broadcasting markets. There are few markets which are not in some sense regulated. Indeed, there are a number of well-known reasons why broadcasting markets do not always work very well, especially where there is only a limited number of television channels.

The potential market failures in broadcasting have been well explored in the Peacock report and several contemporaneous publications. Briefly, the main economic rationale for public broadcasting originally arises from three important features of the broadcasting market: non-excludability, barriers to entry, and its 'public good' characteristics.

Non-excludability – the inability to prevent non-payers from receiving a broadcast – meant that it was not initially possible to charge viewers directly for receiving programmes. Attempts to charge for programmes in the absence of excludability would have led to non-payers 'free-riding' (watching without paying) at the expense of payers. Techniques have been developed which now make direct payment for television possible, but until recently the equipment and support systems were costly. For most of broadcasting history there has therefore been no direct link between audiences and broadcasters via a payment system – a common feature of most other markets. Indirect methods (e.g. via advertising) of financing broadcasting had to be found.

At the same time, technological constraints combined with government policy to restrict the amount of radio spectrum allocated to broadcasting meant that only a limited number of television and radio channels were allowed to operate. If there is only a limited number of advertiser-financed channels then the chances are increased that those channels will all choose to attract the same audience with the same programme types. They will prefer to have a share of the large mass audience than to attract all of a (smaller) potential audience for a minority interest show. The result would be the provision of a fairly limited range of programmes. This effect has been explained by several economists, and is modelled in detail by Owen, Beebe and Manning, among others.[6] It has been used to justify government intervention to ensure that a wider range of programmes is broadcast.

The central weakness of an advertiser-financed system is that it fails to take each viewer's or listener's intensity of preference into account. Television advertisers are primarily concerned with the number of viewers rather than their level of interest or enjoyment of the programme. In a normal competitive market, consumers are able to signal the intensity of their preferences by the amount they are willing to pay for a good or service. This gives producers an incentive to supply goods or services to meet a range of tastes. In broadcasting, until direct payment systems were developed, there was no way that this could happen.

A third rationale for government intervention in broadcasting, even where direct payment is possible, is the 'public good' argument. Broadcasting is very like a pure public good, in the sense that its cost of production is largely independent of the number of people who consume it. The standard example of a public good is national defence. Since it costs nothing to supply the good to any additional consumer, it is inefficient to exclude any consumer who values the good at any positive level. However, if price discrimination is not possible, the producer will have to charge a positive uniform price for the good (sufficient to cover its costs) which will inevitably exclude all consumers whose value for the good lies between zero and that price. This is a possible justification for using a compulsory flat rate licence fee to finance a public broadcaster, even where direct payment systems are feasible. Of course, given the difficulty of deciding what the flat rate should be and then ensuring that the public broadcaster spends the proceeds efficiently, this method may be no more efficient than the pure market system.[7]

Government intervention in broadcasting could also perhaps be justified in terms of wider economic benefits (or externalities) which are unlikely to be captured by a privately operated market-based system. An example of such an external benefit might be the gains that arise as a result of public service programmes leading to a better educated and informed society. Public broadcasters provide a means of ensuring that such programmes are produced.[8]

It will not, however, have escaped the reader's attention that these economic rationales are now less strong than they once were. Many different types of programmes are now provided by the private sector, on an increasing number of channels. It is possible to charge directly for programmes. There are many other sources of information and education in modern society. Even if some of these developments are only in their emergent stages, it seems likely that broadcasting markets will undergo a huge transformation in the 1990s as they become more widespread.

A Narrow Remit?

More careful analysis is therefore needed of the gaps in programming supply that exist now and will continue to exist throughout the 1990s, and which public broadcasters might be asked to fill. Consideration is also needed of how those gaps should be funded. An examination of radio and television schedules in Europe indicates, perhaps surprisingly, that there are few programme types[9] not now provided in some form by the private broadcasting sector. The exceptions are:

- documentaries;
- 'high brow' arts and culture;
- educational programmes;
- programmes for some minority/ethnic interest groups;
- radio drama, documentaries and analysis.

In smaller European markets, private competitors tend to offer fewer programmes of local origin (and more US imports) than public broadcasters. In the larger markets, however, audiences demand local productions and the private operators compete for audiences on this basis. Unless there are other reasons why public broadcasting should include programming similar to that provided by the private sector, there would seem to be a strong case to restrict it to a narrower range of programmes and services than has hitherto been the case.

Rationales for a Broader Remit

There may, however, be reasons for more extensive government intervention in broadcasting than indicated by the above list.

First, there may be industrial policy reasons. Some governments are concerned about US dominance of world film and television markets, for example. US producers, it is claimed, have an advantage over producers in other countries, because of their large domestic market. This helps them recover production costs through home-market sales, allowing them to export programmes to overseas markets at low prices (the marginal cost of each export sale is low). Without government support for film and television production, it is argued, local producers would never be able to compete effectively with US producers. Such support might take the form of direct finance for local production (perhaps via a public broadcaster) or the imposition of maximum quotas on the use of overseas programming material.

While this sort of intervention no doubt creates income and jobs which would not otherwise exist, it also inevitably increases the cost of television in the short term (broadcasters have to replace cheaper acquired material with more expensive locally-produced material). It also may prevent viewers from receiving the programmes they would prefer to watch. This rationale should therefore be examined carefully.

Second, government intervention in broadcasting might, arguably, be required to support creativity and innovation. These might be under-provided in a more commercial environment, perhaps because of an unwillingness of commercial broadcasters to take a long-term view or to make risky investments. The argument for public intervention here would be similar to that used to justify public support for research and development – which (it is argued) private markets tend to under-supply. There is some anecdotal evidence, especially from the US, to support this view.[10] If a particular programme is a success on the main US networks, much effort is expended on attempts to create similar programmes, spin-offs or sequels. Similarly, it is argued that there is an increasing tendency for private broadcasters to devise programmes for specific audiences and advertising markets, rather than to begin with creative ideas and then find a slot suited to them.[11] It is equally true, though, that the real programme successes in the US and elsewhere are often the innovative ideas that break new ground. Certainly in many non-broadcasting markets, competition between private companies acts as a positive stimulus to innovation and service improvements.

Third, some commentators have argued that a narrowly focused public broadcaster would have difficulty in attracting the creative talent to maintain service quality. Commenting on the notion of a 'rump BBC', for example, Barnett and Docherty argued that this:

> is the worst of all possible worlds: it will push the BBC to the margins of British broadcasting (and consequently British society) leaving the commercial stations to clean up on all forms on entertainment.... The result will be a vicious circle of low ratings, low investment and lack of morale, resulting in a fundamental destabilising of the broadcasting system in this country.[12]

If society places a positive value on public service programming, it clearly makes sense to ensure it is effectively provided by skilled broadcasters. However, the prevailing trend in broadcasting is one of greater fragmentation of audiences and specialisation of channels. A greater proportion of production is being sourced from independent companies rather than made in-house by large integrated organisations. A more narrowly-focused public broadcaster could become a well-funded centre of excellence, rather than a rather poorly funded generalist.

Fourth, it may be important for public broadcasters to show a wider programming range in order to justify the continuation of public funding, especially if funds are raised by a licence fee paid by all television set owners. Many public broadcasters would object to the view that their prime responsibility is to address broadcasting market failures. They believe that, to justify a licence fee paid by all viewers or listeners, they have to offer programming to cater for the interests of everyone. This means popular entertainment and drama, even if it duplicates the output of private broadcasters. The result is a rationale for a public broadcasting service which provides everything from local pop radio to classical music stations, from mainstream television entertainment to experimental broadcast drama.

One major difficulty with this argument is that, while it may effectively retain the support of licence fee payers, it also implies a higher licence fee (or more thinly spread resources) than would be the case if a more narrowly focused service were to be offered. It is also a somewhat circular argument – a costly service remit is sustained because of the need to justify the licence fee, which in turn is only needed because of the costly service remit.[13]

There is a danger in restricting the debate to one of extremes. Should public broadcasting offer all things to all men, or should it include only that limited range of output that private broadcasters will never produce? A more pragmatic and productive approach may be to take each programme or service category currently offered by public broadcasters, and assess the extent to which that category (a) would be under-provided in the market or (b) would be provided in a different way (for example, in a shallow or highly trivialised format). Some assessments will be more clear-cut than others. Some programme categories, such as recent release feature films, US-style game shows and non-educational children's cartoons, appear to have little place in the output of a more carefully targeted public broadcaster. The same may well be true of popular music radio stations. Other categories, such as locally produced popular dramas and situation comedies, may have a place in a public broadcaster's schedules if sufficiently differentiated from the output of private broadcasters.

Consulting Viewers and Listeners

Identification of gaps in the broadcasting market which private operators are unlikely to fill does not automatically justify government intervention to fill those gaps. How do we decide on the level of public resources that should be devoted to making serious local dramas, intelligent documentaries, educational children's programmes and so on? How much public money should be spent on television and radio? The missing dimension from the above approach is an understanding of licence fee payers' preferences concerning the expenditure of licence fee income.

A potentially productive means of providing this dimension would be to ask viewers and listeners what value they place on different types of programmes, using the answers as a guideline for public broadcasting policy. Peacock,[14] for example, noted that individuals might derive a general satisfaction from the provision of goods and services to the community at large which is distinct from their own immediate enjoyment of them (support for theatres and museums, for example). Given that the willingness of individuals to pay for these services often depends on whether or not others are prepared to support them, it may be more efficient to finance them publicly than to rely on private or voluntary provision. Peacock used this rationale to support continued public financing of some broadcasting services, although more limited in scope than is typically the case at present. In effect, society would have an 'implicit contract' which ensures that a certain level of cultural provision (in this case broadcasting) is made available to all. Broadcasting would then have a prior claim on resource allocation up to the level implied by the contract.

If this argument is accepted, then a logical extension is to take careful note of consumer opinion in determining the extent and range of the activities of public broadcasters, and how much public finance should be provided to them. In other words, the public needs to be asked what the contract should cover. If licence fee payers are made aware of a range of service mix and cost options, they might well have strong views on whether their public broadcasters should show a wide range of programming or offer a more narrowly defined service. Even if the licence fee is pre-determined, consumers might value an opportunity to express views on how it should be spent – for example, more on sport, less on drama or vice versa. Consumer preferences, in this way, could be used as an input into different resource allocation decisions. In doing so, they would help provide a firmer rationale for public broadcasters' activities.[15]

Institutional Frameworks

Governments can intervene in broadcasting markets in several different ways. Regulated private broadcasting has existed in many countries, particularly in Europe. Examples include ITV in the UK, TFI in France. These channels are usually advertiser-financed, are privately-owned, and run on a commercial basis. The public service content of their output is governed by a licence from government which generally specifies minimum proportions of certain strands of programming and places restrictions on where programmes can be produced. Even the new cable and satellite channels are usually subject to some obligations concerning taste, decency, and advertising content. Other models for government intervention are discussed in Chapter 4.

Given the range of options open to government, public broadcasters need not only to redefine the rationale for public service broadcasting, but they also need to argue the case for its delivery via organisations like themselves. A number of reasons can be advanced in their support.

'If it ain't broke, don't fix it'

Public service broadcasters often have an impressive history. Over the years they have provided a variety of high quality programmes. They have been highly successful in winning critical acclaim and television awards. They have been at the forefront of technological development. They have fostered creative and technical expertise. And for many years they have reached large audiences with their programming. All of this is true, but the real question is not, 'have they done well in the past?', but 'will they be able to adapt to a very different future?' The earlier discussion of changes in broadcasting markets in the 1990s suggests that public broadcasters will at the very least need to consider internal organisational changes, if not a wholesale change in their institutional framework.

'The right to fail'

It is also argued that public broadcasters help stimulate creativity and innovation by providing their programme makers with the right to fail. First, public broadcasters are large enough to spread risks over a number of projects. This means there is more chance of unusual and innovative programmes being financed and broadcast. Second, they are not driven by short term profit considerations, so can allow projects time to develop and mature.

According to the Broadcasting Research Unit, public guidelines for broadcasting should be designed to liberate rather than restrict the programme makers. Public broadcasting:

> protects the freedom to experiment in new broadcasting styles and subjects, to take time and a long breath, to make mistakes in that search, gradually to build up audience from a standing start.[16]

Anecdotal evidence from the BBC, for example, points to successful programmes that initially had low audience ratings. A commercial broadcaster would not have persevered with the development of such programmes, it is implied. Comparison of the BBC with the highly competitive US networks does suggest that programmes are given less time to prove themselves in the US than in the UK. It would be interesting, however to examine overall 'success' and 'failure' rates to establish whether these different approaches to risk and return significantly affect long-term programming performance (a greater turnover of programme ideas might produce more hits in the long run than a policy which allows poor initial performers a second chance).

'A critical mass'

Public broadcasters, it is suggested, provide an essential 'critical mass' for the development of quality broadcasting. The main features of this critical mass are:

- creative staff benefit from being part of a large organisation in which they can exchange ideas and experiences with colleagues;
- a public service philosophy permeates the organisation, and creates a set of shared values and culture;
- a centre of production excellence is created, large enough to support the equipment and technical skills needed for modern broadcasting.

It is difficult to judge how significant these factors are. There are other decentralised broadcasting structures which seem to work well, most notably the use by Channel 4 of large numbers of independent producers. It is possible to obtain easy access to advanced facilities and technical expertise in the private sector. Indeed, as more private broadcasters emerge, so the commercial provision of production facilities and support should expand.[17]

'The importance of integration'

More convincing is the argument that a degree of vertical integration is important if public broadcasters are to compete effectively in future broadcasting markets. Integration of different stages of the broadcasting process is common in the private sector. Large international media companies prefer to control their sources of programme supply as well as their distribution channels. A driving force behind this strategy is the desire to reduce risk – the risk of not being able to sell programmes to distributors or, alternatively, the risk of distributors not being able to secure attractive programme material. A notable difference between the large private operators and public broadcasters is that the former tend to operate autonomous companies (e.g. production, facilities, distribution, sales) within their overall operations, while the latter are usually fully integrated in a single organisation. As a consequence, public broadcasters often have little real idea of the costs and operating profitability of each part of their organisation.

'Goodwill'

Finally, by virtue of their long (for broadcasting) histories, public broadcasters are well-known to audiences – they have high profile 'brand names'. If effective government intervention in broadcasting markets is to continue, then it arguably makes sense to exploit these brand names to the full, rather than to seek alternative models. This begs the question of whether more effective exploitation of those brand names, to the benefit of the taxpayer, might not be more desirable.

There is a clear downside to the institutional framework within which public broadcasting is conducted. Large public sector bureaucracies do not provide an ideal environment for encouraging productive efficiency or rapid responses to changes in the external environment. Some difficult trade-offs therefore remain to be made when evaluating the benefits and costs of different public broadcasting models.

Some Conclusions

This chapter has argued that 'traditional' value judgements concerning the objectives of public broadcasting provide inadequate guidance to broadcasters and policy makers about how to decide what resources should be allocated to public broadcasting as a whole and to the different components of public broadcasting. Broadcasting authorities, in any event, have often underestimated the ability of the public to make sensible choices about the types of broadcasting they would like to receive.

Market failures do provide a number of rationales for government intervention in broadcasting markets, especially to ensure certain types of programmes are provided and, possibly, to encourage risk-taking and innovation. But developments in broadcasting, especially the rapid emergence of new satellite and cable channels, are reducing the importance of these rationales. The new channels are encroaching on territory which was previously the sole preserve of public broadcasters.

Such changes underline the importance of a reassessment of which services and programmes public broadcasters should offer. Programmes should be identified which are unlikely to be provided by the market, but which nevertheless are of value to individuals or to society as a whole. Indications are that public funding should support a narrower range of programmes and services than has hitherto been the case. But any decision to alter radically the remit of public broadcasters needs to be informed by the views and preferences of viewers and listeners, which could provide useful guidelines for government policy and broadcasters' strategies.

The importance of this issue should not be underestimated. Every extra public resource used by public broadcasters to finance programmes that are better provided by the private sector means less resources available for alternative uses elsewhere – either in broadcasting or elsewhere in the economy.

Governments also need to assess whether public broadcasters, rather than other institutional or organisational models, provide the best conduit for government intervention in broadcasting markets. It is insufficient to argue that public broadcasters have been successful in the past. Arguments concerning the role which public broadcasters play in facilitating risk-taking and innovation need to be supported with concrete research, not just anecdotal evidence. If benefits are generated by providing a home for a critical mass of creative talent, and by vertical integration of operations, they are worth supporting as long as they are not swamped by bureaucratic inefficiency and a lack of internal controls. Measures to reduce the costs associated with public broadcasters' operational methods and structures will strengthen the case for their continued existence into the next century.

3 Improved Accountability

The Importance of Accountability

If public broadcasters are to continue to receive public funding, then they will increasingly have to account for how those funds are used. Partly this is a consequence of a general trend to ensure public spending delivers value for money, partly it results from a view that broadcasters have escaped detailed financial scrutiny for too long. Pressure for greater accountability will also mount as the general public, presented with a wide range of apparently free broadcast services by private operators, begins to question the justification for a compulsory licence fee.

The subject of broadcasting accountability is not new. It was discussed by the UK's Annan report:[1]

> the greatest volume of criticism about the present structure has come to us from those who believe that broadcasters have been insensitive in the past to the views expressed by the public and are insufficiently accountable to them.

Public accountability can mean a number of things. It can mean that the broadcaster listens and takes note of the views and preferences of the public. It can mean that there are channels open to the public to express views about programme services, and to seek redress in the event of broadcasters' wrongdoing (for example, if broadcasters misrepresent facts or opinions). It can mean that broadcasters have to account in detail for their expenditure of public funds and the level and quality of service they provide. Accountability of this last type might be exercised on the public's behalf by Parliament or by an agency answerable to Parliament.

Accountability in all these senses has been notable in the past largely by its absence from mainstream public broadcasting debate. Many public broadcasters, for example, are left to regulate themselves. They provide services in accordance with broad objectives, set out in grandly named statutes, directives, charters, or statements of intent (for example the BBC in the UK, NHK in Japan). These documents rarely give detailed guidelines concerning programme and other objectives and obligations. Nor do they contain financial targets or objectives. Formal regulation of programme content is more likely to be applied to private broadcasters than to public broadcasting organisations. In few (if any) cases is performance monitored on a regular and consistent basis.[2]

The shortcomings are not all those of the broadcasters. Governments often try to influence public broadcasters directly or indirectly. It is not unknown for political appointees to command the top jobs in public broadcasting organisations, and for broadcasting policy to change with governments or ministers. In the absence of clear objectives and responsibilities, it is difficult for governments to determine whether or not public broadcasters are performing effectively. Likewise, it is difficult for broadcasters to demonstrate they are meeting their side of a bargain in the absence of any specific agreement between them and the government. Improved accountability should therefore benefit both sides.

Accountability in the Public Sector

A well-documented problem of public sector organisations in general is the difficulty of ensuring they deliver services of the desired quality as efficiently as possible.[3] In the private sector, given effective competition, the interests of the enterprise generally coincide with those of the consumer. Enterprises will make profits if they provide goods and services which consumers want to buy, at prices lower than competing suppliers. Incentives provided by competition help ensure firms operate efficiently and meet consumer demands.

Similar incentives usually do not exist in the public sector. Many public operators are monopoly suppliers of their particular goods or service. Even where public operators face competition, they may be constrained from behaving as if they were in the private sector. For example, they are often faced with a range of conflicting objectives and obligations. These vary from normal commercial objectives (e.g. investing in a new train service must make a reasonable rate of return) to political/social objectives (e.g. train services must be provided to remote communities, even if unprofitable). Often, commercial activities are required to subsidise non-commercial activities. Extensive cross-subsidisation disguises the true cost of providing loss-making services, and might siphon off funds which would otherwise have been available for investment in more profitable opportunities. Management receives blurred signals about where to allocate resources and invest funds.

Public sector organisations also have different incentives structures to those in the private sector. Although there are well-known imperfections in private capital markets which mean inter alia that the interests of shareholders are not always pursued wholeheartedly by managers, the public sector often has even weaker external discipline. The public sector is characterised by a whole series of 'principal-agent' problems (concerning the difficulties encountered when one group – the principals – tries to persuade another group – the agents – to act in the first group's interests). In theory, civil servants in the relevant government departments should be in the best position to ensure public sector organisations act in the public interest. Their effectiveness is hampered by their lack of information and specialist skills, however. They are often generalists with frequent changes in their responsibilities. Moreover, there is the threat of 'regulatory capture'. This is the process whereby those responsible for overseeing a public sector organisation tend to become closely identified with the interest of that organisation. While they may try to act in the public interest they inevitably come to look at the operations of the organisation in its own terms. In such cases, solutions which imply radical changes in existing policies are less likely to be adopted.

Ultimate control of a public sector organisation of course rests with the relevant Government Minister. But Ministers are open to the influences of a range of interests and powerful pressure groups, not to mention their own interest in re-election.[4] All of which suggests that clear public interest objectives are unlikely to be pursued. Or if they are, that they are unlikely to survive for long without being influenced by a host of special interests.

As a result, managers in public sector enterprises often receive a confused set of signals concerning their objectives and how their performance will be measured. In response, they may develop their own objectives which will only coincidentally reflect the public interest. Such objectives might include the enhancement of their own power and position, perhaps by proposing large investment programmes or increased output. Improved service to their customers and increases in productive efficiency may receive lower priorities.

Public broadcasters in different countries have experienced many of these problems. Where they are financed by a mixture of public funds and advertising revenues, their operations are characterised by cross-subsidies, which disguise the real cost of 'public service' programming. Their objectives are often only broadly identified, and may change as broadcasting ministers come and go. Civil servants responsible for broadcasting rarely consider radical changes to the institutions they administer. Financial targets, until recently, were the exception rather than the norm, and few incentives have existed to encourage efficient production. Where public broadcasters have been established with independent governing bodies, as with the BBC, they may have escaped undue ministerial influence, but at the expense of reduced public accountability.

Of particular importance, given the current rapid changes in broadcasting markets, are decisions on the extent to which public broadcasters are expected to participate in new technological and market developments (e.g. DTH, satellite channels and subscription television). Is this part of their broad public service remit or should it be left to the private sector? Will their activities in new markets be judged on purely commercial terms, or will they have to satisfy public interest objectives? To what extent can public funds be used to finance new ventures? There are currently few clear answers to these and similar questions.

Service Specification

Recognition of problems of accountability in the public sector has led to different attempts to deal with them, the most radical of which is to privatise the public sector enterprise and require it to operate as a commercial enterprise. Privatised enterprises, especially if exposed to competition, are expected to become more accountable to their customers and their shareholders, and to improve their productive efficiency. Where competition has not accompanied privatisation, regulation has been introduced in an attempt to reproduce the effects of a competitive market.

Privatisation does not solve the problem of how to finance non-commercial services which the government wishes should be provided. It can however make the method and cost of providing of such services more explicit. For example, some privatisations have been accompanied by the formal imposition of conditions or obligations on the privatised company (e.g. requiring a privatised telephone company to provide a universal telephone service or to set up low price schemes to help users; requiring private bus contractors to provide certain basic service levels and offer specified tariffs). These obligations are usually clearly stated in the form of a fixed-period licence awarded to the privatised company. In other words, there is a contract between government and supplier to provide the specified services.

Similar measures involving more detailed service specification, can be taken to improve public sector accountability. Contracting out of services by local government is now a common feature in the provision of many public services ranging from refuse collection to catering. Bidders are asked to submit the costs of providing the service, the aim being to find the lowest-cost (i.e. most efficient) contractor. Contract documents supplied by local authorities to potential contractors have in general contained very detailed specifications concerning the type and level of service required. Performance of the successful contractor is monitored, and financial penalties are imposed if service quality drops below the specified level. The process of contracting out forces the government authority concerned to formulate a clear description of the service it requires. It also provides a good framework for subsequent monitoring of performance and for corrective action to be taken should performance fall below expectations.

Competitive bidding for contracts, which imposes efficiency incentives on the bidders, is not always feasible. However, it is still possible to obtain some of the benefits of contracting-out – particularly those resulting from a clear service specification – in a non-competitive situation. For example, the UK government is now implementing its so-called 'Citizen's Charter',[5] which aims to make providers of public services more answerable to the public. The Charter obliges public sector enterprises and regulated firms to publish information about the levels and quality of service they are providing. Penalties are to be imposed if the actual service fails to meet target levels. Users (e.g. the public) will in some cases be entitled to compensation.

The Citizen's Charter includes measures like maximum waiting time for treatments in the National Health Service, publication of results achieved by schools, money back to travellers if trains are unacceptably delayed, and targets for first class postal delivery times. It also formalises the powers of the regulators of privatised industries, who will be able to require those utilities to:

- regularly publish a report of key service quality indicators;
- achieve pre-specified levels for some of these indicators;

- make fixed payments to customers in the event of failing to meet certain minimum service criteria;

- introduce codes of conduct dealing with the services offered to customers and the termination of services.[6]

Consumers should be able to use the Charter to lobby for better services from public sector and privatised enterprises. Those same enterprises could turn the charter to their advantage by using it where appropriate to demonstrate the service quality they are providing (i.e. demonstrating to the public that they are doing their jobs properly).

For all these measures to be effective, a number of conditions must be satisfied:

- it must be possible to specify the service required in a contract;

- relevant service quality indicators must be available, in order that performance can be monitored;

- action must be possible in the event of any failure to meet the contract obligations.

The Citizen's Charter has been criticised on the grounds that the service quality targets it sets are not very demanding, and that compensation for poor service is inadequate (often no more than a money-back guarantee). Moreover it is not yet clear whether any additional funds will be available, even if they are needed to improve service quality levels. Nevertheless, some of the basic principles involved are laudable and worth developing.

A Public Broadcasting Contract

Can a concept with the apparently limited ambition (for example) of ensuring British Rail makes adequate announcements about delayed trains have anything of relevance to offer the public broadcasting debate? Probably the main lesson from the above discussion is that it is no longer satisfactory for public broadcasters to work to vague and unclear remits. Whatever definition of public broadcasting is adopted, it is likely that governments will wish to negotiate a more detailed specification of the broadcasters' duties before agreeing to further funding. Although there is the obvious danger of over-intrusive government interference in programming policy, a clearer remit should also be to the advantage of public broadcasters. Clear objectives and obligations will help public broadcasters argue for adequate funds and provide a firm basis for demonstrating to consumers that those objectives are being met.

Defining what those objectives and obligations should be is a more difficult matter. In the previous chapter, it was suggested that publicly-funded broadcasting is likely in future to be more carefully focused than is true of the current output of most public broadcasters. It was also argued that broadcasters and governments need to involve viewers and listeners in determining what that focus should be. Public broadcasting would have a much stronger legitimacy if it could demonstrate the support and appreciation of the public it is meant to serve.[7]

As an input into determining the public broadcasting contract, therefore, ways should be found of:

- establishing what the *public* wants public broadcasting to be;
- giving the public involvement in deciding what is provided.

Sophisticated survey techniques (some of which are already used to assess how particular programmes perform) could be used to help devise the initial contract. Consumers could, for example, be asked to choose between different packages of broadcasting services at different costs, to establish their preferred combination of services and licence fee. The packages would be chosen carefully to reflect realistic possible service combinations.

Provision should also be made for periodic changes in the contract to reflect variations in public preferences and in the broadcasting environment. A good option might be to use the licence fee collection process as a means of asking licence-fee payers to express their preferences as to how some or all of the licence-fee funds should be spent. The public could be asked to rank different programme categories or services, to indicate their own priorities for funding. Alternatively, the public could be asked to allocate their licence-fee to different programme types or to special projects. To begin with, perhaps a proportion of annual funds would be set aside for 'viewers' choice' programming. Broadcasters would be obliged by the contract to act according to this guidance.

Having established the broad nature and scope of the service to be funded, the problem of adequately specifying a contract must be addressed.

There are well-known difficulties in drawing up contracts for broadcasting services.[8] It is, for example, difficult to define and measure programme quality (as opposed to quantity). A list of programme requirements can only specify with any precision an incomplete range of programme attributes (such as number of hours of programmes of each type to be broadcast each week, time slots when they should be shown, etc). If broadcasters' programme obligations are extended to include a subjective element concerning quality and nature of content, then the scope for the contracting parties to interpret such obligations in a flexible (and uncertain) manner increases. Resolution of disputes over contract terms becomes more complex and costly. There are also dangers in over-specification of contracts, which might impose unwarranted costs on broadcasters (trying to comply with detailed regulations) and stifle creativity and innovation.

But the potential advantages mean that public broadcasting contracts merit serious evaluation. In the UK, the recent Channel 3 licences include a number of specific programme and other conditions which licensees must meet. Similar conditions could be applied to public broadcasters. A typical contract might include:

Service Obligations

- number of television channels, radio stations and other services to be provided;
- broad remits for each channel/station;
- broadcasting hours and geographic coverage for each channel/station;
- transmission/signal quality standards.

Programme Obligations

- minimum hours of different types of programming (e.g. average hours per week of news, current affairs, drama, documentaries, children's programmes);
- minimum hours of locally produced programmes;
- prime-time scheduling requirements;
- minimum amount of local and regional programming;
- any specialist minority interest or language requirements.

General Obligations

- standards of taste, decency;
- accuracy and impartiality;
- cater for the interests and tastes of viewers and listeners not adequately provided for by other broadcasters.

Additional obligations might be considered. For example, requirements could be specified for distribution of budgets between different broad categories of programmes, especially if based on surveys of viewer preferences. Contracts could also direct the public service broadcaster to conduct detailed periodic surveys of audience preferences, and to demonstrate how those preferences are built into programming and funding decisions. Contracts should be periodically reviewed as the broadcasting environment changes.

It would be wrong to believe that a service contract as specified could provide an exhaustive and all-inclusive blueprint for public broadcasting. No contract can adequately express requirements for creativity and innovation, for example. But there are enough elements of the broadcasting service that can be incorporated in a contract to make the exercise worthwhile. It may also be possible to use service contracts to disentangle the public service elements of a public broadcaster's activities from the more commercial elements. The purpose of public funding would become more transparent, and broadcasters could be given more freedom to pursue their remaining commercial activities with less government intervention.

Service Quality Indicators

The use of performance indicators to monitor the services provided by privatised industries and public enterprises was noted earlier. They help year-on-year comparisons of service levels, and provide benchmark comparisons with similar organisations. The mere fact of their publication might provide an incentive for embarrassed managers to improve performance. A challenge for public broadcasters will be to develop more meaningful service quality and performance indicators which can be used to reassure viewers and listeners that they are providing value for money.

The considerations involved are:

- the value of the information produced compared with the costs of its production;
- whether performance targets should be set and, if so, at what level;
- what action can be taken in the event that targets are missed.

Performance indicators would certainly include the key elements of any contract, as described above (number of hours of news, drama, etc.). These data will be easy to compile from programme schedules, and provide the minimum information necessary to check that the broadcaster is meeting its contract. Indicators will also be needed which describe quality. Measurement of inputs (quality of actors, amount spent on sets and costumes, etc.) might give a partial indication of quality but the costs of compiling these data could exceed the value of the information produced. Much better would be measurements of output. These might include:

- *audience ratings* – which measure the popularity of programmes, and cannot be ignored by public broadcasters.
- *audience reach* – which measures the number of people who take advantage of the service at some time during the week. This is an important indicator of how well the public broadcaster is providing programming of value to all licence fee payers.
- *audience approval indicators* – which would measure how well-liked individual programmes are by audiences in general and by those at whom they are particularly aimed.

It would be a mistake to judge public broadcasters solely on audience ratings or share, especially if their role has been redefined to reduce the importance of mass-appeal programming. It should however, be possible to devise a measure of the ratio of actual ratings to 'expected ratings'. Expected ratings would take into account the nature of the programme concerned, its scheduling time – and the likely strength of competing programmes.[9]

The data base for all three types of performance indicator already exists in the UK and many other countries. Production of these indicators on a regular basis should be relatively inexpensive. Additionally, regular surveys might be requested to explore in more detail what audiences think of particular programmes or overall scheduling policy. Many broadcasters have developed sophisticated techniques for identifying the factors which create successful programming and for judging whether programmes, given their attributes, have performed as well as they should have done. Public broadcasters should be encouraged to adopt these techniques, if they have not already done so, and should be required to publish their survey results. More generally, governments should ensure that public broadcasters do not get away with selective publication of performance data. A review of many European public broadcasters' annual reports, for example, shows that current published data concentrate mainly on success stories, and provide a very incomplete picture of each broadcaster's overall performance. Other indicators should measure the efficiency of the organisation (in terms of suitable measures of output per unit of input) and its interface with viewers (e.g. number of complaints received, efficiency with which they are handled).

The question of target setting is more complex for it requires an answer to the question, what is the optimal level of service quality? There will be a point beyond which the costs involved in improving service quality exceed the benefits to consumers of the improvement achieved. In the absence of a market mechanism, a judgement of the optimal level could be based on surveys of consumers. Service levels delivered by private broadcasters might also provide useful benchmarks. Targets will also need to take account of past performance in order to avoid placing unrealistic demands for rapid improvement on the public broadcaster.

Finally, performance indicators and targets are of little value if no action is taken to reward good performance or to penalise poor performance. It should be possible to devise systems by which staff and management rewards are affected by performance, providing an internal incentive to meet targets. In the longer run, the level of public funding made available to public broadcasters could be tied to an assessment of past performance.

Some Conclusions

The funding of public broadcasters is coming increasingly under the public expenditure microscope. Governments concerned with controlling public expenditure are insisting that public sector enterprises deliver value for money and are more accountable both to civil servants and to their customers, the general public. As part of this movement, public sector enterprises are being asked to enter into more formal service contracts or agreements, and to publish information about the level and quality of service they provide. Public broadcasters are unlikely to escape these developments and, indeed, may be able to turn them to their advantage.

Recognising the need for clearer contracts and service performance indicators does not solve the problem of how to implement them, or provide guidance on the optimal service levels required. As a general principle, though, contracted services should draw their legitimacy from the nature and scope of public broadcasting that the general public (the licence fee- payers) would like to support. Likewise, service quality indicators should concentrate on measuring public approval for the service and programmes produced. Formalised contracts will help ensure that important questions concerning the future scope of public broadcasters' activities are properly addressed. It may even be possible to 'decouple' the public service aspects of a public broadcaster's output from the more commercial elements.

Although contracts and performance indicators improve the accountability of public sector enterprises in the sense that they help ensure a certain level and quality of service is delivered, they do not in themselves ensure that service is delivered as efficiently as possible. Publication of performance indicators which measure productive efficiency (e.g. output per head, average cost per unit of output) may provide an indirect incentive for the enterprise to become more efficient over time. But information asymetries – the public enterprise itself will be in the best position to know its own current and potential costs of production – mean that government officials and the public will find it difficult to judge whether the enterprise is performing efficiently or not. Privatisation, which replaces government control with the disciplines of shareholder control, and contracting out, by which service contracts are awarded to the lowest cost operators, both incorporate extra efficiency incentives. Even so, it has been necessary to devise additional methods of encouraging efficiency in those privatised utilities which face little or no competition. In the next chapter, methods which might be used to encourage the efficiency of public service broadcasters, are examined drawing on the experience of regulated utilities.

4 Encouraging Efficiency

Economic Efficiency

What do we mean when we argue that public broadcasting policy should encourage efficiency? Economists generally refer to three types of efficiency:

- *allocative efficiency* – measures at any given time the extent to which scarce economic resources are being channelled to their highest valued use; the economically optimal allocation of resources means that there is no reallocation – either to other users or uses – that would have a higher value to society;

- *dynamic efficiency* – measures the extent to which, over a period of time, as market conditions change, resources can be channelled to their highest valued use (hence allowing society to benefit from innovation and technical advancement);

- *productive efficiency* – measures the extent to which for any given unit of output, the lowest cost combination of inputs is being used.

In effect, economic efficiency can be described as that state of affairs in which, given the value of the resources available, one has taken advantage of every available opportunity to increase the economic welfare of consumers through the provision of larger quantities of outputs, better products, or a mixture of outputs better adapted to consumer preferences. This is a necessary condition for the maximisation of general welfare (it may not be a sufficient condition, because other social, moral and philosophical conditions may need to be satisfied).

A key objective of broadcasting policy should therefore be the pursuit of all three types of efficiency. One approach is to encourage the development of a free market in broadcasting. The key elements of a market are tradeability, price, and information. Resources can be transferred from low to high value uses via transactions in the market. Prices act as a signal to users to tell them whether or not to buy or sell a particular resource. Information helps buyers and sellers make their trading decisions. The competitive process also encourages individuals and organisations to search for new ideas and products, for that is how they can gain a competitive advantage over their rivals. Firms are encouraged to produce their output as efficiently as possible, otherwise lower-cost rivals will win sales through their lower prices.[1]

Where competitive markets for various reasons cannot exist,[2] or traditionally have not existed, governments and economists have sought ways of reproducing their beneficial effects. Some of their approaches are of relevance to the public broadcasting debate.

In the following discussion, the different approaches are classified under three broad headings:

- economic regulation;
- internal markets;
- market mechanisms.

Economic regulation is a term used to describe the regulatory mechanisms set up to control the activities of privatised utilities which are not subject to sufficient competitive pressures. The principal objective of such regulation is to replicate the forces of competition, to persuade the regulated firm to behave as if it were operating in a competitive market. According to William Baumol:

> the task of regulation should merely be to seek replication of the behaviour patterns which would have emerged if competition had been more effective. In other words, regulation should never be more constraining than market forces and should impose no rules inconsistent with the normal workings of free markets.[3]

The main feature of such regulation is that it should control prices and/or profits of the regulated firm to ensure that the firm does not exploit its monopoly power at the expense of consumers. At the same time, the form of regulation chosen should allow the regulated firm to earn a sufficient rate of return to continue in business and to provide for essential future investment. Finally, regulation should provide incentives for the regulated firm to improve its internal efficiency.

In the UK, the major privatised utilities (British Telecom, British Gas, the Water Companies, and the Electricity Distribution Companies) all have their own industry-specific independent regulators (Oftel, Ofgas, Ofwat, Offer). The concept of independent regulation is also being extended to the control of those enterprises remaining in the public sector. In the UK, an independent regulatory body is to be set up to regulate the Post Office. In the rest of Europe, independent regulators have been established (at the insistence of the European Commission) to regulate the activities of the state-owned telephone companies.

Elements of the different methods of economic regulation, and the concept of an independent regulator are likely to be important components of any future public service broadcasting arrangements.

Internal markets are designed to benefit organisations which, though they are not necessarily operating in a competitive external market, have the scope to improve their internal resource allocation and productive efficiency. Large organisations can be thought of as economies in miniature, with many transactions taking place each day between different divisions or departments. For the most part, there is no need to formalise such transactions with written contracts and prices. Indeed for most organisations the transactions costs in so doing would far exceed the benefits. For very large organisations, however, especially those with significant or complex internal transfers, it may be beneficial to introduce more formal buyer/seller relationships. A recent example is given by the UK government's reforms of the National Health Service.

The development of more structured internal markets could well be of benefit to large public broadcasters.

Market mechanisms is a term, somewhat loosely used here, to describe a range of other approaches that might be taken to introduce elements of the market process (trading, prices, information) into activities where they have hitherto been absent. A common application of market mechanisms involves the creation of tradeable permits or licences to use or exploit resources which have previously been allocated by an administrative process or which have been freely available (rationed by queuing). Their aim is to capture the benefits that price signals and tradeability can bring in the resource allocation process. Such schemes have been designed to ration access to airport landing slots (the creation of landing rights which can be bought and sold by airlines wishing to use an airport) and to control vehicle access to urban areas. Tradeable permits for the use of radio frequencies have been introduced in New Zealand (allowing the purchase and sale of frequencies needed to operate telephone and broadcasting services).[4] In many western countries licences to broadcast radio and television services are tradeable, even if only via the takeover of the existing licence holder by another company. Market mechanisms are also being used to improve pollution control via the creation of tradeable permits.[5]

The following sections examine the scope for incorporating some of these approaches to encourage the efficient provision of public broadcasting.

Economic Regulation

Privatised utilities which are not exposed to sufficient competition are subjected to economic regulation to ensure that they do not earn monopoly profits and that they have an incentive to operate efficiently.[6] Control of monopoly profits is either imposed directly, in the form of a limit on the rate of return which the regulated firm can earn, or indirectly via a price cap. The latter, common in the UK, places a ceiling on allowed price increases, and can be applied to the prices of individual goods and services, or to a basket of goods and services.

Efficiency incentives can be provided in several ways. If rate of return-style regulation is being used, 'regulatory lag' might help encourage firms to be more efficient. Regulatory lag refers to the delay between any increase in the regulated firm's profits above its allowed rate of return (due perhaps to improved efficiency) and an order from the regulator that its prices must be reduced to bring profits back into line with its allowed rate of return. If there were no regulatory lag, the firm would have little incentive to cut its costs –

any gains in profits would be immediately removed by enforced lower prices. So-called incentive regulation is an alternative approach. This provides for a bargain to be struck between the regulated firm and the regulator which allows the firm to retain a share of any increased profits resulting from efficiency improvements, which may be more or less narrowly specified.[7]

The UK system of price-cap control provides an automatic efficiency incentive.[8] Prices of the regulated firm are typically linked to an external index in a 'price-cap formula' (often known as an RPI-X formula, because prices are generally allowed to increase in line with the retail price index less an amount 'X' which reflects the scope for reasonable productivity improvements or other unit cost changes). The formula is applied unchanged for a number of years. Hence the regulated firm has an incentive during that time to cut costs, in the knowledge that it will be able to retain the resulting profits.[9]

Principles of economic regulation would be applied to public service broadcasters in several ways.

The least obvious way is to control their profits. Few public broadcasters are established as profit-making organisations. They are expected to spend, more or less, the funds they receive each year. They do not have to make a return for shareholders. However, the efficiency incentives incorporated in some regulatory mechanisms would be of value. The principles of price-cap control are most suited to public broadcasters, as price-caps could easily be applied to licence-fee payments. An indexed licence fee could be used to provide an incentive for public broadcasters to reduce their costs, or at least to contain them to increase only in line with general price increases. Indeed, this is the approach adopted in the UK, where the BBC's licence fee is currently indexed to the RPI.

The main issues to be considered in applying a price cap to public broadcasting fees are:

- the index to which the licence fee should be tied;
- the period between price-cap reviews;
- the scope for cost improvements;
- the scope for incorporating additional efficiency incentives in the mechanism;
- implications for service level and quality.

In all regulated industries in the UK there has been a keen debate concerning whether the relevant index for price-control formulae is the RPI, some other general price index such as the GDP deflator, or a specific cost index (reflecting the costs faced by the industry concerned). 'Cost pass-through', by which some cost elements are allowed to be passed on directly to the consumer, has been incorporated in some price control formulae. A discussion of the arguments is continued in Oftel's recent consultative document on the regulation of BT's prices,[10] and a comprehensive account of the UK price-control formulae is given in a recent paper by D.R. Glynn.[11]

The question for broadcasting is whether trends in broadcasting industry costs are (a) markedly different from trends in the RPI, and (b) exogenous to the broadcaster concerned (a major public broadcaster might, for example, have substantial influence over industry-wide labour and other resource costs). Unless convincing arguments are produced on both points, the case for using the RPI or its equivalent would seem strong.

The period between price-cap reviews and the scope for cost improvements are largely empirical issues. An advantage of relatively infrequent reviews, however, is that it removes part of the discretionary element of public funding and increases the certainty that a given level of funding will be available for a number of years.

More difficult is the question of appropriate efficiency incentives. The BBC, for example, currently has a cap placed on its licence fee based on RPI. In effect this is a total revenue cap, which provides little incentive for the BBC to seek efficiency gains beyond those required by the cap itself.[12] Indeed, it may even be in the BBC's interests to inflate its costs in order to convince government to provide more funding when the formula is next reviewed. The scope for the BBC acting in this way can presumably be limited by requiring a periodic independent review of its finances. But such exercises are costly, and the BBC will always have an advantage over the government or its advisers in its access to the cost and other information on which any judgement must be based.

Efficiency incentives would be improved if success in cutting costs benefitted the broadcasters themselves. This might be accomplished by allowing managers to retain part of any surplus themselves, or perhaps, by making certain management initiatives conditional on achieving efficiency targets. For example, if the public broadcaster reduces the costs of its core service by more than is implied by the price cap, it could be allowed to invest in specified additional high-budget programmes, expand its service coverage (a new radio station, perhaps) or diversify into other business sectors or geographic markets.

Some drawbacks of price-cap control should be noted. Another way of increasing prices is to cut the quality of the service while charging the same for it. Price-cap control in itself contains nothing to prevent this happening. Nor does it make any allowance for an increase in costs to cover improvements in service quality – perhaps as a result of technological change. Hence regulators are increasingly recognising the need to monitor the service quality provided by their regulated firms. Price-cap control might also depress investment. Without any specification as to the level of investment required from the regulated firm, there may be an incentive for that firm to drop desirable but not particularly profitable investments – such as quality enhancing improvements. If the price-cap control does not make sufficient allowance for future investment needs, then the expenditure might not take place. This is an issue of particular relevance to broadcasters in view of the likely high investment requirements if advances such as high definition television are to be made widely available.

Another issue of some importance is the relationship between a public broadcaster's commercial revenues and its public funds. Price-control formulae are usually determined with reference to the regulated enterprise's projected revenues and costs. If any increase in commercial revenues simply feeds back into a tighter cap on the licence fee via this process, then the public broadcasters will have little incentive to seek commercial opportunities. Conversely, governments will be concerned to ensure that resources paid for by the public via the licence fee are not used by public broadcasters to cross-subsidise their commercial activities.

One final component of economic regulation which deserves serious consideration in the broadcasting context is the creation of an independent industry-specific regulator. As noted in Chapter 2, public broadcasters have largely been self-regulating in the past. If measures are taken to increase public broadcasters' accountability, then creation of an independent regulator responsible for monitoring their performance is a logical complementary step. Independent regulation has a number of advantages:

- independence of government: UK regulators are answerable to Parliament, and so are less likely to be influenced overtly by day-to-day political considerations;

- independence of the regulated enterprise: there is a clear and sometimes confrontational relationship between regulator and regulated firm, which diminishes the danger of regulatory capture;

- defined objectives: independent regulators can be given defined objectives, and their actions have to be justified in these terms;

- industry knowledge: an industry-specific regulatory body can accumulate information and expertise which increases its ability to determine whether the regulated enterprise is justified in its demands (say) for higher prices or profits.

It seems likely that an independent broadcasting regulator would be able to exert more effective influence and control over a public service broadcaster on *behalf of the public* than would either the relevant government department or an appointed governing body. Such a regulator could be given responsibility for administering the funding of public broadcasting, monitoring service quality, and vetting financial and other information requested from the broadcasters. The regulator would also have a duty to research public attitudes to the broadcasters' output and reflect these in its decisions. The regulator would not determine the level of public funding to be allocated to the public broadcasters, but would advise the government at each periodic funding review, and would monitor the public broadcasters' financial performance thereafter.

Some cautionary notes should be sounded before leaving this subject. First, regulation costs money. There is a temptation often for regulators to extend their empires and to adopt a more interventionist stance than is strictly justified. Second, regulators are only effective if they have adequate information from the regulated enterprise. UK experience in regulating privatised utilities underlines the importance of ensuring the regulator has an adequate flow of information. Third, regulators, notwithstanding the above remark about regulatory capture, can also become too closely associated with the interests of the regulated enterprise. Efforts will need to be made to avoid these dangers if an independent broadcasting regulator is established.[13]

Internal Markets

There is much scope for the application of internal market principles to existing public broadcasting structures. Some public broadcasters, such as the BBC, have already made progress in this area.

The broad principles of an internal market are:

- an organisation is divided into a number of separate entities (divisions, departments or even separate subsidiaries) that are tied together in a trading relationship (buying from or selling goods and services to each other);
- prices are set for the internal transfer of such goods and services;
- each entity in the organisation is required to cover its costs (possibly including a profit element) via the prices it charges for its goods and services;
- individual entities are given the option to buy goods and services from outside the organisation, if they can get a better price;
- incentives are provided to encourage entities to maximise their income net of costs.

In a broadcasting organisation, for example, the production facilities house might charge programme producers for the use of its services. They in turn might 'sell' their completed programmes to the television channel scheduler. If the system works well, it should provide incentives for the various parts of the broadcasting organisation to operate more efficiently, and should also produce valuable information for senior management decisions on resource allocation.

For an internal market to be effective, however, some important conditions have to be met:

- there has to be a good costing system in place, otherwise pricing and allocation decisions will be based on inadequate and misleading information;
- some constraint must be placed on the ability of entities to source goods and services externally. If an outside quote is cheaper than an internal quote based on average fully allocated costs, then an unconstrained decision maker would decide to source externally. However,

the external quote might well be higher than the marginal cost of providing the good or service internally (reflecting high internal fixed costs and low variable costs). In the short term, at least, economic efficiency is best served by sourcing internally. A system will need to be put in place to avoid the wrong decisions being taken;

- there has to be an effective incentives system to encourage efficiency. For example, if programme producers know that if they succeed in cutting their expenditure, then their budgets will be reduced the following year, then there will be little incentive for them to do so.

Television New Zealand is one public broadcaster which saw the benefits of internal markets, and introduced them at an early stage of a radical reorganisation of the business.[14] The BBC's 'Producer Choice' initiative is adopting similar principles.

The creation of an internal market will help public broadcasters examine the relative efficiency over time of each element of their operations. If it becomes clear that external suppliers are operating at a significantly lower cost, then an eventual decision to close down the internal unit and source externally can be taken.

Market Mechanisms

The incorporation of other market mechanisms in the provision of public broadcasting would involve more radical change than the measures discussed so far. Three main options can be identified:

- market-based allocation of radio frequencies, including those used by public broadcasters;
- competitive bidding (by all broadcasters) for public broadcasting funds;
- direct payment, by consumers, for public broadcasting services.

Market-based radio spectrum allocation has already been introduced in New Zealand.[15] Spectrum rights can be bought and sold, and the owners of those rights can use the spectrum for whatever purpose they choose, subject to restrictions on allowable interference. (e.g. for telephony, radio, television, telemetry and so on). The opportunity cost of using each part of the spectrum (i.e. its highest valued alternative use) is reflected in the price users have to pay for it. As a result, spectrum should find its way into the hands of those who value it most highly – leading to efficient resource allocation.

If such a system were to be more widely adopted, how would it affect public broadcasters? If they had to bid for spectrum along with all other users, the full opportunity cost of the radio frequencies they occupy would immediately be revealed (at present, public broadcasters are in the privileged position of having free access to valuable frequencies).[16] The immediate impact would be a rise in public broadcasters' operating costs and further pressure on their funding. Although this might be desirable in economic terms, it is unlikely to be attractive either to governments who would be faced with immediate demands to increase licence fees or to the broadcasters (for obvious reasons). It would, however, be possible to gain some of the economic advantages of a market-based radio spectrum system if public broadcasters were 'grand-fathered' (i.e. given free) the rights to their existing radio frequencies and were then allowed to sell those rights (or buy new ones) in the market. This would encourage public broadcasters to assess carefully the benefits and true costs of some of the services they offer.

In the UK, for example, the BBC would have to trade-off the benefits of (say) retaining its Radio 1 and 2 national radio stations and the costs of so doing (operating costs *plus* any foregone revenue, i.e. the revenue it would have got from selling the frequencies to a private operator).[17] Forcing public broadcasters to make this sort of calculation would increase their own aware-ness of the true costs of their services and thus help generate a more efficient allocation of scarce radio spectrum.

Competitive bidding for public broadcasting funds is a concept discussed in the Peacock report and has also been implemented in New Zealand.[18] A criticism of traditional public broadcasters is that they have not had to compete for the public element of their funding.[19] This may arguably have led to a lack of innovation in public broadcasting ideas, or have reduced incentives to produce quality programmes in a cost-effective manner.[20] It may have resulted in an establishment-dominated public broadcasting culture, to which outsiders are denied access.

A radical departure from the current system would be to allocate public funds to any producer or broadcaster (whether publicly or privately owned) with an approved proposal for public service programming. In the UK, for example, competitive bids for funds might be requested from the BBC, ITV, Channel 4 and 5, satellite channels and from independent producers. Peacock suggested the establishment of a Public Service Broadcasting Council (PSBC) to perform this function. According to Peacock, the programmes funded by the PSBC would:

> be likely to be a narrower group than 'everything the BBC at present does' but a larger group that what has been called rather gracelessly 'an arts and cultural affairs ghetto'.[21]

This system seems to work well in New Zealand. After a review of New Zealand broadcasting policy in 1988, a new government body, NZ on Air, was established. NZ on Air collects licence fee payments and uses them to finance public service television and radio programmes and services. Part of the fund is used to finance universal transmission (subsidising transmission to remote parts of the country) and part is used to support Maori broadcasting services. The rest is distributed as follows:

- For television: NZ on Air invites proposals for individual pro-grammes or series from independent producers or from the main broadcasters (state-owned TVNZ or private TV3). Each proposal must have the agreement of one of the broadcasters to transmit it, and each proposal must already have attracted some external funding.
- For radio: NZ on Air provides a block grant to the two main national public radio stations (equivalent to the BBC's Radios 3 and 4). What little is remaining is available for proposals from other radio stations.

Although the criteria used by NZ on Air to decide which proposals to fund are less explicitly set out than might be expected, programmes generally have a strong New Zealand content and range from arts documentaries to a locally produced soap opera.

The system is not seen as a complete success by all commentators however. Because the television broadcasters have been given very few specific pro-gramme obligations (bidding for NZ on Air funds is entirely voluntary) there is a concern that too few 'public service' programmes are shown on television, particularly the more serious types of current affairs, analysis and docu-mentary programmes.[22] New Zealand, moreover, is a somewhat special case. Most of the public broadcaster's funding came from advertising revenues (84 per cent) rather than licence fees, even before the new system was introduced. The New Zealand model may therefore require some modification before it could be applied to public broadcasting in those markets where licence-fee income still accounts for a major part of the public broadcaster's revenues.

Moreover, if this model is adopted, it is difficult to envisage a convincing rationale for the continued existence of public broadcasters in the form we know them today. TVNZ is still state-owned in New Zealand, but it has been set commercial objectives and has few explicit public service obligations. To all intents and purposes it could be a private broadcaster. The key public broadcasting role has been taken on by NZ on Air, the body responsible for disbursing funds. The same would be true in Europe if the system were to be adopted here.[23]

A less radical variation of competitive bidding might, however, be intro-duced by breaking up the larger public broadcasting organisations into their constituent parts. It is not necessarily obvious, for example, why television and radio operations should be part of the same single organisation. Formed into separate companies, they could negotiate their own contracts with government, introducing a competitive element into the distribution of funds. Likewise, it might be possible to create competing public television services, with each service having one channel, or perhaps being responsible for several channels but for only part of the week.

The benefits from increased competition for funds would clearly need to be offset against potential cost increases – for example, any lost economies of scale and scope, or any increased transactions costs involved in negotiating contracts with several different services.

Direct payment by the public for public broadcasting is the third market mechanism to be discussed, and this would also involve a radical transformation of the public broadcasting scene. Evidence from around the world shows that subscription television is technically and commercially feasible. But there is no clear evidence yet that the public would be prepared to pay in sufficient numbers for a viable mixed public television and radio service of the type commonly provided by traditional public service broadcasters.[24] Subscription television first developed in the US, with the spread of cable networks to many areas of the country.[25] Cable operators initially charged relatively low fees to viewers to provide 'basic' packages. These usually consisted of the main national and local terrestrial channels, plus some out-of-area local channels. It was realised, though, that viewers would pay higher subscription fees for certain types of programming unavailable on the general entertainment networks, namely premium films and some sports events. Hence the development of specialised premium subscription channels such as HBO and the Disney Channel.

As Chapter 1 noted, subscription is already a major source of television income in some countries, and will continue to grow in the next decade. Even so, there are still doubts concerning the implications of subscription for public broadcasters. The potential problems are:

- it is not clear whether a subscription-financed public service/general entertainments channel would be viable – none has yet emerged in developed television markets and competition from commercial general entertainment channels means that viewers might be slow to volunteer payment for something they can already get 'free'.

- even if viewers would be willing to pay a sufficient amount to support a varied public service channel, there are significant costs associated with a switch to subscription funding for public broadcasters:

  - a subscription-financed public broadcaster would face far greater uncertainty over future income levels than it does at present;

  - there would be substantial costs associated with subscription management and the installation of receiving equipment in subscribing households;

  - there would be a significant loss of universality, as some viewers would inevitably choose not to receive the service.

Some of these problems could be addressed by modifying programme strategy to attract more subscribers. But this might entail a significant change in the nature and mix of programming shown. Where subscription might be a valuable option for public broadcasters would be in the generation of additional revenues which could help support the main core service. For example, public broadcasters might explore setting up new satellite channels to exploit the subscription market, or encrypt the off-peak hours of their main terrestrial service. The widespread public acceptance of pay-TV could, ironically, also help public broadcasters demonstrate the 'good value' provided by the licence fee (which will appear relatively inexpensive compared with monthly subscriptions for, say, film or sports channels. According to Patricia Hodgson, the BBC's head of policy and planning:

> [the licence fee] is the cheapest and most cost-effective form of direct payment. The growth of satellite subscription puts it in perspective. In the next century, it could well be taken for granted as the 'standing charge' for the heartland public service channels, with the audience choosing to top-up with subscriptions to add-on services (BBC and other) for more of what they value most.[26]

This statement may contain an element of wishful thinking, but it does indicate a recognition that public broadcasters will need to demonstrate the value for money they deliver to their customers, compared with competing pay channels.

Some Conclusions

Whatever the remit given to public broadcasters, there is an unanswerable case for ensuring they produce their service as efficiently as possible. This means the encouragement of internal productive efficiency, and also the pursuit of efficient resource allocation between competing broadcasters and between broadcasting and other uses.

Various mechanisms could be used to provide public broadcasters with effective efficiency incentives. One option is a licence-fee indexation formula, modelled on the type of price-cap regulation typically used in the UK to control the prices of privatised utilities. Care would need to be taken to ensure that such a formula did not produce adverse service quality incentives or prevent desirable capital investment. It would generally be preferable to fix the licence fee formula for a period of several years, to provide public broadcasters with greater funding certainty and freedom from more frequent government intervention. A related option would be the establishment of an independent broadcasting regulator, modelled after Oftel or Ofgas, to monitor and control the public broadcaster's activities.

Public broadcasters' internal efficiency incentives could be improved by the establishment of a system of internal markets and the contracting-out of some services. At the very least, such a process will enable the broadcaster to collect detailed information on industry-wide production costs, which will provide a useful benchmark for its own performance.

More radical use of market mechanisms could yield the biggest efficiency gains, but will also provide public broadcasters with their greatest challenge.

Competition for public broadcasting funds and the increased exploitation of subscription revenue, in particular, would call into question the rationale for the existing institutional framework for the provision of public radio and television.

5 Options for Public Broadcasters

Accountability and Efficiency

Like motherhood and apple pie it would be difficult to object to the twin aims of more accountability and efficiency for public broadcasters. Public broadcasters, whatever their remit, should ultimately account for their actions to the providers of their funding. They should be encouraged to make use of their funds as efficiently as possible. If some of the suggestions in this paper are implemented, public broadcasters will be in a stronger position to face the future. Their remits will be more clearly defined and, importantly, will have greater public legitimacy. They will have an improved incentive to be more efficient. In return for greater accountability public broadcasters should be able to negotiate greater funding certainty.

The achievement of improved accountability and efficiency, however, only partially resolves the difficult issue of what society should expect from its public broadcasters. It also sidesteps the issue of affordability – as Chapter 1 indicated, public broadcasters will inevitably face significant financial pressures during the next decade, which will impact on the scope and quality of service they can provide. How best should they cope with such pressures?

In this final chapter, two options are identified, which are meant to represent contrasting outcomes. As will be seen, there are potentially serious drawbacks to both options, which underline the difficult policy decisions that have to be taken by governments and public broadcasters alike.

The 'Core-Service' Option

As described in Chapter 2, one option, strongly supported by those who argue that governments should limit their intervention to the correction of market failures, is for public broadcasters to adopt a more narrowly or carefully targeted programming remit. In its purest form, this would limit public broadcasters to a 'gap-filling' exercise. A reduction in public funding might be associated with this option if it implies a significant cut back in the scale and scope of public broadcasters' operations.

A concern expressed by public broadcasters is that such a policy would lead to a vicious downwards spiral of underfunding and declining audiences. The service provided would be increasingly marginalised, and find it difficult to attract the creative talent needed to produce quality radio and television. Whilst such claims are probably exaggerated – in the wider broadcasting market, a notable recent trend is towards more specialised channels which are successful even with relatively low audiences – it should not be ignored entirely by policy makers.

That the danger might exist underlines the importance of asking licence-fee payers themselves to help determine what types of service the public broadcaster should provide. The public might well sanction a wider range of programming than would strictly be implied by the 'gap-filling' approach described earlier, but this is not certain. It would also be difficult to ensure that this approach produced an optimal level of public broadcasting, especially if government were simply to pick an arbitrary licence fee (say the existing level) and ask the public how they would like it spent. A more sophisticated survey technique, which gave the public choices between different levels of licence fee and different combinations of services consistent with those levels might get nearer to the right answer.

Chapter 2 identified several reasons for supporting the view that public broadcasters should offer more than a very limited core service. The encouragement of creativity, innovation and risk taking in all types of programming might justify giving public broadcasters a wider remit. Even so, it is likely that funding constraints will force unpleasant choices on public broadcasters, making it difficult for them to continue to provide 'something for everyone' unless new funding sources can be exploited.

A 'Wider Service' Option

In contrast with the core-service option, there exists the option of providing a much broader service level. Public broadcasters could be encouraged to provide a comprehensive range of programmes via a variety of delivery methods. They would not face any restrictions on the scale and scope of the services they offered. They could be asked to remain at the forefront of new technology, and play a full role in new broadcasting markets. Given that public funds are unlikely to be sufficient in themselves to fund the necessary scale of expenditure, this option would need to be accompanied by a high degree of commercialisation. In this scenario, public broadcasters could be asked to pursue commercial objectives, subject to the constraints imposed by their public service contracts. The presumption would be that the public service contract provided funds for a proportion of the broadcaster's output, the remainder (the commercial programming) being financed by advertising or subscription.

This option would appear best suited to those public broadcasters which already receive a substantial proportion of their total funds from advertising revenues or other commercial sources. Explicit accounting of the public service element of their operations would be needed, and adequate arrangements for funding that element would need to be established. Broadcasters would then have the freedom to maximise their revenues from the more obviously commercial parts of their schedules.

How would the public service programming be identified, costed and funded?

NERA has had to address this question in Singapore, where a new system of regulating and funding public service television is being developed. Singapore Broadcasting Corporation (SBC) currently broadcasts a mixed television and radio service which, like most public service broadcasting, contains some programming that would be equally well placed on private commercial services. SBC is partly funded by a licence fee, partly by advertising. Advertising is accepted in all programmes, even those which have been defined as public service programmes.[1]

The current preferred proposal is for SBC to agree a contract with the government to provide these programmes in pre-determined amounts, with funding based initially on the full opportunity cost of the programmes. This is calculated as the production cost of the public service programmes, plus the opportunity cost of not transmitting commercial programmes (the advertising and sponsorship revenues that would have been earned, less the costs of the programmes) less any advertising and sponsorship revenues earned from the public service programmes. Different options are being explored for building efficiency incentives into the public service contract. The current preferred method is a three year contract with the initial year's funding calculated as described above, and the remaining two years' funding linked to an external price or cost index.

What of an organisation, like the BBC, which is still wholly publicly funded? If the 'SBC' definitions of public service programming were to be mapped into the BBC's services, a large proportion of the BBC's output would not qualify for funding. The 'SBC' approach could work only in its current form if the BBC were to be allowed to accept advertising. The principles of an agreed contract, and funding linked for a period to an external index could still be applied to the BBC, however. The issue of how much of the BBC's existing services deserve continued public support would then need to be addressed.

Privatisation

If the 'wider-service' option is chosen, then the door is opened for privatisation. The potential benefits of privatisation of state-owned industries are well known.[2] Where public service broadcasters have access to mixed funding (licence fee and advertising), the rationale for retaining public ownership of the organisation will be much reduced if well-defined public service contracts can be developed for the publicly-funded element. Government influence over programming content could be exercised via the public service contract. If this is working effectively, then government ownership of the broadcasting enterprise arguably is not necessary. Privatisation will then provide the former public broadcaster with the flexibility and access to funds to develop its commercial broadcasting activities, while creating strong incentives for efficient production. Consideration would need to be given to issues of market dominance and competition, and it may be necessary to restructure the enterprise in advance of privatisation, perhaps into separate radio and television operators, or into separate television channels. However, broadcasting markets are in most countries now increasingly open to competition, which should reduce substantially the threat of anti-competitive behaviour by the privatised broadcaster.[3]

Public broadcasters like the BBC, which are wholly funded by licence fees or grants, are a different matter. Privatisation of the BBC as a single entity in its current form, for example, would achieve few of the advantages conventionally associated with a change from public to private ownership. It would still be dependent for the vast bulk of its income from a single public contract. Its value to potential investors would depend almost solely on the likely continuation of earnings from that contract. There would be little scope to introduce competition for public broadcasting funds without significantly reducing the BBC's flotation value. Consequently, the government would face problems (in determining the true cost of public broadcasting and whether the BBC is operating efficiently) identical to those it faces today.

A Middle Way?

Is there a middle way for public broadcasters, between the doldrums of a narrow core service and the stormy commercialisation associated with privatisation? If there is, would it be a good policy choice?

Clearly there *are* ways of enhancing the core service option without necessarily increasing the burden placed on public funding. An uncontroversial incremental step would be to encourage public broadcasters to sell their programmes to other broadcasters. Any income received helps either to improve service quality or to reduce the call on public funds. Exploitation of programming via merchandising, video sale or rental, recorded cassette sales, etc, could also be encouraged. It would be for consideration, though, whether public broadcasters should undertake such activities in-house or be asked to license the exploitation rights to private companies. The latter may be preferable if it is concluded that a very different set of skills is required for effective exploitation.

More difficult to resolve is the issue of the provision of new broadcasting services (such as a new satellite channel), either as stand-alone operations or as joint ventures. In theory, public broadcasters should be encouraged to exploit their assets to the full. Any income generated will help reduce the need for public funding. Relevant assets might include the studio facilities they have built for their main public broadcasting activities or, even more importantly, their programming archives. The large European public broadcasters in particular have built up substantial programme archives over the years, the potential value of which could be significant, once any remaining copyright and performance rights issues have been resolved. One option would be for public broadcasters to sell their programme rights to the highest bidder, hence realising any locked-in value for re-investment in their main public service. If the tenders are transparent and fairly conducted, this would not have a distorting effect on the private broadcasting sector (all private broadcasters would be free to bid) and would in theory maximise public broadcasters' income from those programme rights. The drawback for public broadcasters, however, is that the sale of programme rights to other broadcasters may in the long term strengthen the private broadcasting sector, and depress viewing of the public channels.

Some public broadcasters are therefore enthusiastically exploring the idea of recycling their programme material on their own new services (or indeed expanding their operations with the addition of extra satellite/cable television channels and radio stations). Examples of ventures proposed by public broadcasters in Europe include new satellite channels run by the German public broadcasters, and the EBU's Eurosport and Euronews projects. In New Zealand, state-owned TVNZ has already invested in a private three-channel pay TV service and in a new telecommunications company. Singapore Broadcasting Corporation is considering investment in a pan-Asian satellite service.

Here the public policy issues are more complex. First, such ventures involve public broadcasters expanding way beyond their original, albeit vaguely defined, remits. Second, although they may be justified *ex ante* in commercial terms, the risk (if they fail) is inevitably borne by public funds. A failed satellite venture may be paid for in terms of reduced mainstream programme quality. Third, the scope exists for the public broadcaster to distort competition in the broadcasting market. For example, archive programmes might be provided to a new channel at below their opportunity cost, giving the channel an unfair advantage compared with potential competitors. The public broadcaster might be able to use its dominant position in terrestrial broadcasting to secure exclusive contracts for its satellite offshoot, again with the aim of shutting out potential competition.[4] Finally, the public broadcaster could provide promotion for its satellite channel on its terrestrial services. If those terrestrial services do not accept other forms of advertising, this could be especially valuable. If such activities are to be encouraged, broadcasting regulation needs to ensure that public broadcasters compete fairly and do not place public funds at risk.

Perhaps a more fundamental problem with the 'middle way' approach is that it might succeed only in helping public broadcasters postpone their day of reckoning. Finding new ways to generate extra commercial revenues (perhaps through the introduction of peripheral subscription services) might help provide a marginal increase in total income. But this may not be enough in the longer term to offset the effects of a squeeze on either or both licence-fee funding or advertising income. This danger is probably greatest for those public broadcasters who depend on advertising income for a substantial share of their total revenues. Unless they change their programming policy, their audience and revenue share will crumble away. But a change in their programming policy starts to undermine their reason for existence.

Radical Change at the BBC?

Licence-fee funded broadcasters like the BBC are probably in a better position, so long as they can retain a broad political support for public funding at pretty much its current level. The BBC's best bet may well therefore be to build from its present base (give or take a few of its more expendable services) rather than to plan for more substantial change. Any shortfall in licence fee revenues would need to be made up from income generated by new commercial ventures. Even so, some parties are likely to press for more radical change, including more extensive use of subscription and even privatisation.

Is privatisation of the BBC worth serious consideration? This question could only be properly answered after a much more detailed analysis of the benefits and costs than has been possible in this paper. One thing is clear, however, a privatised BBC would look very different to the animal we currently know and love. The rest of the UK broadcasting industry would also be immensely altered. For a start, if privatisation of any of the BBC's activities is to be considered, then it will also be necessary to 'commercialise' (i.e. allow access to advertising revenue or other commercial income) those parts. Candidates for privatisation frequently mentioned in the past include Radios 1 and 2 and local radio stations. It has been quite fairly pointed out by the BBC that these would not, on their own, reduce significantly its need for public funding. However, their privatisation would be consistent with a more carefully targeted public service remit.

The really radical approach would be to transform the BBC into a commercial enterprise which could accept some amount of advertising and pursue subscription income, subject to a more clearly specified public service contract. Privatisation on this scale would create a large (in international terms) commercial broadcaster, with a strong home market, valuable existing programme assets, and the benefit of operating in the English language. It would be a chance to create a private UK-based world-force in broadcasting, able to capitalise on a well-known brand image and to compete alongside US producers for a share of the expanding world media-market. The UK has no equivalent operator and, arguably, is foregoing valuable potential export revenue as a result.

Of course the short term impact of this option on private UK broadcasters would be immense, especially in the private television sector. Advertising on the BBC would mean less revenue for its commercial rivals. While Channel 3 might be strong enough to survive, there would be some doubt about the continued viability of Channel 4 and the new Channel 5. The precise scale of impact would, of course, depend when and how gradually advertising is introduced on the BBC. In an expanding overall market, the later and slower the change is made, the less dramatic will the effect be. Moreover, the effects of competition for revenues from the BBC on other operators could be mitigated by making available some public funding for their programmes out of the total licence-fee pot.

Some constraints could also be placed on the BBC's ability to tap into the various sources of revenue. A privatised BBC might, for example, be required to take the following form:[5]

- BBC 1 – a mainstream advertising-financed popular channel, with some public service programming paid for out of public funds by a clearly specified 'public service contract'.[6]
- BBC 2 – a mainly subscription-financed specialist channel.
- Radios 3 and 4 – financed entirely by public service contracts.
- Radios 1 and 2 – financed by advertising.

The privatised BBC would then be free to operate as many other television and radio services as it wanted (both in the UK and overseas) and for which it could obtain licences.

Some additional public funding might be available for other UK radio and television operators, with competitive bids being invited for funds. A newly strengthened broadcasting regulator would monitor all parts of the broadcasting industry, and a new public service funding body would be required to award and administer the public service contracts.

Some Conclusions

To return to the theme of Chapter 1, revenue and cost pressures will force inevitable change on public broadcasters around the world. The challenge is for broadcasters and policy makers to find new methods of broadcasting organisation which preserve the best elements of public service, without undue burden on public funds, and which allow the broadcasters to adapt and compete with their fast-growing competitors.

This paper has argued that measures can be taken by public broadcasters to strengthen their positions, regarding both accountability and efficiency. However, even with a strong political commitment to maintain public broadcasting, it is likely that public broadcasters will encounter funding constraints during the next ten years.

Two contrasting options were identified:

- a 'core-service' option, in which public broadcasters concentrate on filling in the gaps left by the private sector;
- a 'wider service' option, in which public broadcasters provide much broader programming services in direct competition with private operators.

The first option brings with it the danger of increasing marginalisation, which might be partly offset by seeking greater public legitimacy, and a demonstration of real accountability. To fund the second option, it is almost inevitable that public broadcasters will need to exploit commercial revenue sources, including advertising and subscription. Given this, it makes sense for many public broadcasters (especially those already financed in part by advertising revenues) to be set commercial objectives, subject to well defined and funded public service contracts for their 'non-commercial' programme output. If the second option is chosen, then privatisation of the public broadcaster would be a logical development.

The BBC is in a rather different position to the majority of its public counterparts from elsewhere in the world, in that it depends wholly on public funding. Privatisation of the BBC would make little sense unless accompanied by a wholesale change in the BBC's methods of finance (which in turn would affect the entire UK broadcasting sector). This risk of large scale disruption would only be worth taking if privatisation is thought to be the only way of unlocking the BBC's immense potential as a world force in broadcasting and as a major UK export earner. But the costs could also be immense.[7] Whether or not privatisation is on the agenda, an assessment of the benefits and costs of a more commercially oriented BBC should be a central part of the forthcoming charter review. Also important will be a strengthened regulatory framework, which should encourage the BBC to exploit profitable commercial opportunities, while safeguarding the public (from paying for the BBC's commercial failures) and other broadcasters (from unfair competition).

Notes

Introduction pp. ix to xiii
1. Public broadcasters' are defined here as television and radio broadcasters owned by the state. They might be financed wholly by public funds (e.g. via a licence fee or grant from general taxation) or by a mix of public funds and commercial revenue (e.g. advertising). Some public broadcasters (e.g. RTVE in Spain) are financed almost entirely by advertising.

Chapter 1 pp. 1 to 11
1. For a discussion of the emergence of terrestrial television in Europe, see R. Foster and S. Holder, *Europe's Television in the 1990s* (Economist Intelligence Unit, 1990).
2. E.g. restrictions on which products can be advertised and when advertisements can be broadcast.
3. Direct payment for radio is unlikely to be significant, partly because the transaction costs are likely to be high relative to the value placed on radio programmes by listeners. It may be possible to develop some specialist pay-radio services, however, perhaps using satellite delivery.

Chapter 2 pp. 12 to 25
1. 'The Economics of Broadcasting and Government Policy', *American Economic Review*, lxi (1966) pp. 440–475.
2. *Report of the Committee on the Future of Broadcasting* (Cmnd 6753: March 1977).
3. Consumers do not always know best. For example, there would probably be a consensus that serious drug addicts should be protected from their own cravings, children should be protected from persuasive advertising etc. But the general rule usually holds.
4. *Report of the Committee on Financing the BBC* (Cmnd 9824: July 1986).
5. *Report of the Committee on Financing the BBC*, p. 133, para 592.
6. B. Owen, J. Beebe and W. Manning Jr., *Television Economics* (Canada, 1976).
7. For a discussion of subscription television and the theory of public goods, see Minasians' 'Television Pricing and the Theory of Public Goods' and Samuelson's 'Public Goods and Subscription TV: Correction of the Record,' *Journal of Law and Economics*, lxxi (1964) pp. 81–3. The Peacock Report also summarises the arguments (paras 554–6).
8. As Martin Cave notes, however, this rationale is 'often applied elastically and without serious attempt at substantiation': M. Cave, 'Financing British Broadcasting', *Lloyds Bank Review*, clvii (July 1985) p. 28.
9. Classified by subject matter.

10. For example, see J.G. Blumler, *Multi Channel Television in the US: Policy Lessons for Britain* (ITV Association, 1989).
11. Of course, in itself this is not necessarily a bad thing as long as the programmes that result are of good quality and are well-liked by their target audiences.
12. S. Barnett and D. Docherty, *The Peacock Debate in the UK* (Broadcasting Research Unit, 1986).
13. Note also, that audience research e.g. as quoted by Barwise and Ehrenberg in *Television and its Audiences* (London, 1988) suggests that all viewers from time to time watch 'minority' programmes; a minority broadcaster could still claim majority support.
14. *Report of the Committee on Financing the BBC*, para 129.
15. For most public goods, paid for out of general taxation, it is infeasible to consult consumers on the level of resources they would allocate to the provision of that good. Where broadcasting is paid for via the licence fee – an hypothecated tax – the opportunity does exist.
16. *The Public Service Idea in British Television – Main Principles* (Broadcasting Research Unity, 1986).
17. This will be especially so if, as seems likely, private broadcasters adopt a 'publisher' model for their operations, with very few production facilities of their own.

Chapter 3 pp. 26 to 35

1. *Report of the Committee on the Future of Broadcasting*, p. 31, para 4.6.
2. Samuel Brittan described one aspect of this situation: 'Some BBC officials are so used to the idea of being financed by what is virtually a tax on the possession of a television set, that they do not realise how privileged and unusual their position is, and how much in need of continuing and detailed justification. No other consumer products are financed in this way, certainly not books, or newspapers, or entertainment. Even the National Theatre and Covent Garden have to finance themselves in some part from box office takings': S. Brittan, 'The Fight for Freedom in Broadcasting', *Political Quarterly*, dviii (1987), p. 9. In defence of the BBC, their 1991/92 Annual Report contains a section headed 'Public Accountability'. Moreover, in his foreword to the Report, the BBC's chairman describes the hallmark of the BBC as 'distinctiveness, quality, efficiency, accountability and demonstrably meeting public need' (BBC Annual Report 1991/92, p. 3).
3. See for example the discussion in J. Vickers and G. Yarrow, *Privatisation: An Economic Analysis* (MIT Press, 1988) pp. 27–44.
4. Indeed, public choice economics often thinks in terms of 'vote maximisation' as opposed to 'profit maximisation'.
5. *The Citizen's Charter: Raising the Standard* (Cm 1599: London, 1991).
6. *Competition and Service (Utilities) Act 1992* (HMSO, London, 1992)
7. This does not mean that public service broadcasters should simply pursue audience ratings. It means that they should seek to satisfy the tastes and preferences of different categories of viewers and listeners, and provide the overall public service audiences wish in general to receive.
8. See, for example, the discussion by R. Foster and K. Cheong in G. Hughes and D. Vines (eds), *Deregulation and the Future of Commercial Television* (The David Hume Institute, 1989) pp. 91–125.
9. Statistical techniques are available which can help calculate such ratios.

Chapter 4 pp. 36 to 48

1. Markets usually need to be regulated to ensure that effective competition is sustainable and to provide a means of addressing market failures (for example, ensuring there is an adequate flow of information between sellers and buyers).
2. For example, in the case of natural monopolies, such as the supply of water.
3. William J. Baumol, 'Modified Regulation of Telecommunications and the Public Interest Standard', unpublished monograph.
4. Traditionally, allocation of the radio frequency spectrum and its broadcasting use has been administered by a centralised command and control mechanism.
5. See, for example, *The Use of Market Mechanisms in the Regulation of Air Pollution* (NERA, 1986), prepared for the UK Centre for Economic and Environmental Development.
6. For the standard discussion of economic regulation, see A. Kahn, *The Economics of Regulation* (USA, 1970).
7. For a summary of types of incentive regulation, see J.H. Landon and S.M. St Marie, 'Embodiments of Incentives in Regulation', presented to the Euro-American Conference on Organising and Regulating Electric Systems, 1990.
8. For a comparison of price cap and rate of return regulation see for example M. Beesley and S. Littlechild, 'The Regulation of Privatised Monopolies in the UK', *Rand Journal of Economics*, xx, No.3 (1989) pp. 454–72.
9. It should be noted that UK regulators recently have appeared more willing to intervene during the price control period to change the formula if the regulated firm's profits are causing public concern.
10. *The Regulation of BT's Prices* (UK Office of Telecommunications, January 1992).
11. D.R. Glynn, 'The Mechanisms of Price Control', *Utilities Policy* (April 1992) pp. 90–9.
12. If the BBC wishes to increase output, it may have to reduce unit costs further than implied by the licence fee index.
13. Note that in some countries including the UK, independent broadcasting regulators already exist, with responsibilities for regulation of the private broadcasting sector. Indeed, the Chairman of the UK's Independent Television Commission has suggested that the ITC's role could be expanded to include regulation of the BBC.
14. TVNZ also experienced some of the problems, and was forced to introduce central controls on outsourcing decisions, to avoid significant underutilisation of its facilities.
15. For a discussion of the New Zealand system, see NERA's report on *Management of the Radio Frequency Spectrum in New Zealand* (NZ Ministry of Commerce, 1988).
16. Note that in the UK private television and radio companies have been prepared to pay large amounts for licences which, in effect, give them a right to use certain specified radio frequencies.
17. This assumes, of course, that ownership rights to those frequencies are vested in the BBC.
18. See *Report of the Committee on Financing the BBC*, p. 148, para 687.
19. Indeed, if the licence fee is regarded as a hypothecated tax, they have not had to compete with any other public expenditure claims for their resources.
20. Anecdotal evidence suggests this is rather a harsh criticism. Moreover, it is equally possible to argue that lack of competition might have helped creativity and innovation (see the discussion in Chapter 2). It is unlikely, however, to have reduced costs.

21. *Report of the Committee on Financing the BBC*, p. 130, para 579.
22. On the other hand, people watch more television in New Zealand than ever before, which may indicate that most of the public approve, if not all politicians and broadcasters.
23. Alan Budd has noted that the Peacock Committee's PSBC will remove the rationale for public ownership of the BBC: 'At that stage (i.e. after the adoption of the PSBC proposal) it will be difficult to see why the BBC should remain in public ownership. The Committee has, in effect, set a timetable for its eventual privatisation': A. Budd, 'The Peacock Committee and the BBC', *Public Money*, vi, No. 3 (December 1986).
24. See for example Booz Allen, *Subscription Television: a Study for the Home Office* (HMSO, 1987).
25. Originally prompted by the poor quality of terrestrial broadcast reception.
26. P. Hodgson, 'New Meanings and Roles for Public Television', conference paper, 1991.

Chapter 5 pp. 49 to 56

1. The broad approach in defining a public service programme in Singapore has been, as suggested earlier, to consider (a) which programme types would probably not be broadcast (or would be broadcast in reduced amounts) by a private commercial broadcaster and (b) which of these are perceived to be of continuing value to the Singapore public and nation. The second question was answered by referring to objectives set out by the Singapore government.
2. See for example C. Veljanovski, *Selling the State: Privatisation in Britain* (London, 1987).
3. In view of the potential influence on public opinion that broadcasters might exercise, the implications of private ownership for the accuracy and impartiality of programming would need special attention. Media concentration and cross-ownership regulations might require strengthening.
4. The European Commission has been asked, for example, to investigate the joint venture set up by the European Broadcasting Union to operate a satellite sports channel.
5. The BBC's assets would include goodwill, programme archives, physical assets, and licences to use specified radio frequencies for television and radio.
6. Part of the terms of the contract might be that the publicly-funded programmes should contain no advertising breaks.
7. Even the liberal economist Samuel Brittan has stopped short of advocating privatisation of the BBC:

> To some, privatisation may then be the logical next step. But I would hesitate to comment myself. We are not establishing a broadcasting system in a new country. History and tradition do matter; and the continued public ownership of the BBC will do little harm so long as an eagle eye is kept open for privilege and favouritism. (S. Brittan, 'The Fight for Freedom in Broadcasting', *Political Quarterly*, dviii (1987) p. 14.

Bibliography

Barnett, S., and Docherty, D., *The Peacock Debate in the UK*, Broadcasting Research Unit Working Paper, (London, 1986).

Barwise, P., and Ehrenberg, A., *Television and its Audience* (London, 1988).

BBC Annual Report and Accounts 1991/92 (BBC, 1992).

Beesley, M. E., *Privatisation, Regulation and Deregulation* (London, 1992).

Booz Allen and Hamilton, *Subscription Television: A Study for the Home Office* (London, 1987).

Brittan, S., 'The Fight for Freedom in Broadcasting', *Political Quarterly*, dviii (1987), pp. 3–20.

Broadcasting Research Unit, *The Public Service Idea in British Broadcasting, Main Principles* (London, 1985).

Budd, A., 'The Peacock Committee and the BBC: Liberal Values Versus Regulation', *Public Money* (December 1986) pp. 29–33.

Cave, M., 'Financing British Broadcasting', *Lloyds Bank Review*, No. 157 (July 1985), pp. 25–35.

Centre for the Study of Regulated Industries, *Regulated Industries: the U.K. framework* (April 1992).

Coase, R. H., 'The Economics of Broadcasting and Government Policy', *American Economic Review* dvi (May 1986) pp. 440–475.

Crandall, R., 'Regulation of Television Broadcasting, How Costly is the "Public Interest"?', *Regulation* (February 1978) pp. 31–39.

Ehrenberg, A., and Mills, P., *Viewers Willingness to Pay* (Broadcast, 1990).

European Institute for the Media, *Europe 2000: What Kind of Television* (Manchester, 1988).

Federal Communications Commission, *Broadcast Television in a Multichannel Marketplace*, OPP Working Paper Series No. 26P (USA, June 1991).

Foster, R., and Holder, S., *Europe's Television in the 1990s: Growth Opportunities or Regulation*, The Economist Intelligence Unit Special Report No. 2041 (London, 1990).

Glynn, D.R., 'The Mechanics of Price Control', *Utilities Policy*, Vol. 2, No. 2 (April 1992).

Green, D., Centre for Policy Studies, *A Better BBC: Public Service Broadcasting in the '90s*, Policy Study No. 122 (London, 1991).

Home Office, *Broadcasting in the '90s: Competition, Choice and Quality* (Cm 517: London, 1988).

——, *Television Licence Fee (Management Summary)* (London, 1990).

Hughes, G. and Vines, D., *Deregulation and the Future of Commercial Television* (David Hume Institute, 1989).

Institute of Economic Affairs, *Regulators and the Market* (London, 1991).

ITV, *A Response to the Government's White Paper: Broadcasting in the '90s: Competition, Choice and Quality* (London, 1989).

Kahn, A., *The Economics of Regulation: Principles and Institutions*, Vol. i (USA, 1970).

Milligan, S., *What Shall We Do About the BBC?*, Tory Reform Group (London, 1991).

NERA, *Management of the Radio Frequency Spectrum in New Zealand*, Ministry of Commerce (New Zealand, 1988).

——, *1992 and Beyond ... Options for ITV* (London, 1988).

Owen, B., Beebe, J., and Manning, Jr, W., *Television Economics* (USA, 1974).

Report of the Committee on Financing the BBC (Cmnd. 9824: July 1986).

Report of the Committee on the Future of Broadcasting (Cmnd. 6753: March 1977).

Report of the Royal Commission of Inquiry, *Broadcasting and Related Telecommunications in New Zealand* (September 1986).

Sadler, J., *Enquiry into Standards of Cross-Media Promotion* (Cm. 1436: March 1991).

Samuelson, P., 'Public Goods and Subscription TV: A Correction of the Record', *Journal of Law and Economics* (No. 71, 1986) pp. 81–83.

Veljanovski, C., *Freedom in Broadcasting* (London, 1989).

——, *Selling the State: Privatisation in Britain* (London, 1987).

Vickers, J., and Yarrow, G., *Privatisation: An Economic Analysis* (USA, 1988).

The David Hume Institute

The David Hume Institute was registered in January 1985 as a company limited by guarantee: its registration number in Scotland is 91239. It is recognised as a Charity by the Inland Revenue.

The objects of the Institute are to promote discourse and research on economic and legal aspects of public policy questions. It has no political affiliations.

The Institute regularly publishes two series of papers. In the **Hume Paper** series, previously published by Aberdeen University Press, the results of original research by commissioned authors are presented in plain language. **The Hume Occasional Paper** series presents shorter pieces by members of the Institute, by those who have lectured to it and by those who have contributed to 'in-house' research projects. From time to time, important papers which might otherwise become generally inaccessible are presented in the **Hume Reprint Series**. A complete list of the Institute's publications follows.

Hume Occasional Papers

25   Investment Managers and Takeovers: Information and Attitudes *E. Victor Morgan and Ann D. Morgan*
26   Taxation and Mergers Policy *John Chown*
27   Evidence from, The Scottish Office, The Edinburgh University Centre for Theology and Public Issues and Mr D. Henry
28   The Building of the New Europe: National Diversity versus Continental Uniformity *J. E. Meade*
29   The Control of Mergers and Takeovers in the EC *Robert Pringle*
30   How Level a Playing Field does Company Law Provide? *Robert Jack*
31   The Nestlé Takeover of Rowntree *Evan Davis and Graham Bannock*
32   The Power of the Lobbyist: Regulation and Vested Interest, *Michael Casey*
33   Takeovers and Industrial Policy: A Defence, *Graham Bannock and Alan Peacock*
34   The Contemporary Relevance of David Hume, *Robert Pringle*
35   The Remuneration Committee as an Instrument of Corporate Governance, *Brian Main and James Johnston*

Books
The Deregulation of Financial Markets
edited by Richard Dale, Woodhead-Faulkner, London, 1986
Governments and Small Business
Graham Bannock and Alan Peacock, Paul Chapman, London, 1989
Corporate Takeovers and the Public Interest
Graham Bannock and Alan Peacock, Aberdeen University Press, 1991
Social Policies in the Transition to a Market Economy: Report of a Mission to the Russian Federation organised by the United Nations January 1992
Michael Hay and Alan Peacock, Alden Press, Oxford 1992

Hume Reprints
1   The 'Politics' of Investigating Broadcasting Finance *Alan Peacock*
2   Spontaneous Order and the Rule of Law *Neil MacCormick*

Further details of publications may be obtained from:

The Secretary, The David Hume Institute, 21 George Square, Edinburgh EH8 9LD. Tel 031 650 4633: Fax 031 667 9111.